THE MOON OVER CRETE

THE ISLE OF CRETE

THE MOON OVER CRETE

by
Jyotsna Sreenivasan

Illustrations by Sim Gellman

HOLY COW! PRESS · DULUTH · MINNESOTA · 1994

ISBN 0-930100-58-1

We gratefully acknowledge *New Moon: The Magazine for Girls
and Their Dreams* (Duluth, Minnesota) for publishing selected
excerpts from this book.

Publisher's Address:

Holy Cow! Press
Post Office Box 3170
Mount Royal Station
Duluth, Minnesota 55803

Distributor's Address:

The Talman Company, Inc.
131 Spring Street, Suite 201E-N
New York, New York 10012

This project is supported, in part, by a grant from the National
Endowment for the Arts in Washington, D.C., a Federal Agency,
and by generous individuals.

Acknowledgments

Many people helped and encouraged me with this book. I would like to thank: my parents, Vimala and V.V. Sreenivasan; my mother-in-law, Sharon Winstein; Hannah Liebmann of the Center for Partnership Studies; and my husband, Mark Winstein, who gave me wonderful advice and support.

To all the girls and boys,
and women and men,
working to live in partnership
with each other.

Table of Contents

Chapter 1

After School

*L*ily ran home from the bus stop, almost blinded by the tears starting to form in her eyes. She hoped her mother would be home. She had to tell someone!

She unlocked the front door and dropped her backpack at the foot of the stairs. "Mom!" she yelled. She strode through the living room into the kitchen. No one was there. Maybe Mom was outside in the yard. Lily looked out the back and side windows, and saw only a few almost bare trees and a leaf-covered lawn. "Rats. I have to rake that stupid yard again."

She bounded upstairs. Maybe Mom was on the phone or something. But both bedrooms and the study were empty. She saw the answering machine's red light blinking in her parents' bedroom, and turned the knob to hear the messages. "Sorry I'm not home yet, Lily," her mother's voice said against a background of rustling papers. "They scheduled a last-minute meeting. Call me as soon as you get home."

The next message was from her father, who was at a conference in Phoenix. "Hi, Geeta and Lily. The weather's great here, but I can't enjoy it without you two. I'll call you later. Take care of yourselves."

Lily dialed her mother's work number, which she knew by heart. She had to wait a long time for the receptionist to get her mother out of the meeting.

"Hi, sweetie, did you just get home?" Mom was using her super-nice voice, because she felt guilty for not being home.

"Mom, that mean kid Chuck was out there again, when we were getting on the bus. He came up real close to me and—and—" Lily started crying. "He gave me a picture of a naked woman from a dirty magazine! I crumpled it up and threw it at him. Then he called me a bitch! And none of the other kids said anything! He just walked away and no one said anything. When we got on the bus Lauren sat down beside me like always and just started talking about some new hat she was going to get!" Lily sobbed into the phone, wiping her face with the back of her hand.

"Oh, that's awful, Lily! But I'm glad you threw the picture at him. I'll call the school again tomorrow. They should have teachers out there when you kids are getting on the bus!"

"They do have teachers, Mom! But they were over by the doors, talking. Chuck didn't make any noise or hit anyone, so they didn't notice him."

"Well, I'll be home soon and we can talk more. Will you be OK for another hour? There's some soup in the fridge. You can have one cookie too. And remember to practice your flute—you have a lesson tomorrow.

"Okay. See you soon."

Lily hung up the phone and plodded downstairs. She opened the fridge and peeked into the soup pot. "Yuck! Squash soup." She closed the door, grabbed three cookies, and plopped onto the couch in the living room.

Should she do her homework first? Or practice her flute? Or rake leaves? She felt drained and depressed after another encounter with Chuck.

She picked up the remote control and flicked on the TV. Something called "The Dating Connection" was on, which her mother never liked her to watch. The women wore short skirts and high spiky heels. Lily had tried on a pair of pink shoes like that last weekend at the mall, and they hurt! The salesclerk had told her she looked "sweet" wearing them.

The women on TV tossed their long puffy hair back and forth as they smiled big smiles at the camera. Lauren was talking about getting a perm like that as soon as she turned 12. Last week she'd bought a disposable razor and wanted Lily to practice shaving their legs.

The phone rang. Lily jumped up to answer it. "Hello? Oh, hi!" It was Lauren. "I'm just watching TV. And eating cookies. Yeah, I know I shouldn't be eating anything. How long did you stay on your diet, though? That's what I thought, so don't start talking to me about not eating."

Lily settled back on the sofa with the cordless phone, and turned the volume down on the TV. She hoped Lauren had called to talk about Chuck, but she wanted Lauren to bring it up herself.

"I saw what Chuck did to you again today," Lauren began.

"Yeah. Why does he do that?"

"I don't know. He's weird. Just forget about it, Lily. Don't let it bother you."

"You think so? What should I do?"

"Don't do anything. My mom says, with some guys, there's nothing you can do. You just have to ignore their bad points."

Lily wasn't sure what Lauren meant by "don't

do anything." "But Lauren, when someone gives you a picture like that—what am I supposed to do? Put it in my notebook and say 'thank you'?"

Lauren giggled. "Maybe you should! He wouldn't expect that, anyway." Lauren paused, then said, "I think Chuck's kind of cute, anyway. Maybe he just has a crush on you!"

"That's disgusting!" Lily exploded. "I can't believe you'd say something like that, Lauren!"

"Come on, Lily, you've got to admit he's sort of good-looking. Mom says a lot of guys are just shy, and they do things like that to get a girl's attention."

"Lauren, if Chuck thinks I like this attention, he is really stupid!" Lily shouted over the phone. "All I ever do is yell at him!"

Lauren sighed. "What're you getting so huffy about? Calm down."

Lily sighed too, and turned the volume back up on the TV. She and Lauren didn't seem to be able to have a good conversation anymore—Lauren would start saying really crazy things. Lauren turned her TV on too. They started comparing what they thought of the women's clothes, and whether the men were cute or not, and what all the questions and answers meant. She was still on the couch with the TV on when her mom,

Geeta, got home.

"I'm so tired!" Geeta groaned as she kicked off her shoes and flopped onto the sofa. "Turn that silly show off, Lily, and hang up the phone. Is that Lauren? Tell her hi for me. Did you have some soup?"

"I have to go, Lauren. Mom says hi." She switched the phone to "off" and laid it on the table. "You know I hate squash, Mom. Why do you make me eat it?"

"It's good for you. Besides, it's in season. I guess I should get up and throw a couple of bowls of it in the microwave." She continued to half-lie on the couch, her briefcase handle still in her hand.

Lily reached over and rubbed her mother's neck. "Looks like you had a long day. How about if I make us some popcorn?"

"Hmm. Sounds good. Maybe we should have a fun supper tonight. What do you think of burritos?"

"Yeah!"

Geeta went upstairs to change her clothes, and Lily went into the kitchen to rummage around the fridge. She found tortillas, cheese, some left-over refried beans from the burritos they'd had a few days ago, and salsa. She spread the beans on the tortillas, rolled them up, and put them in the microwave while she grated the cheese.

"This thing with Chuck is really getting out of hand," Geeta said as she walked into the kitchen in a pair of gray sweats. She sat down at the table and sighed sadly. Lily knew she was missing Dad—he was away almost one week out of every month now on business.

"Here, hand me the cheese and grater," Geeta said. "I'll do that. Why don't you cut up some of that lettuce in the fridge?" Lily handed her the cheese and opened the fridge door. "I hate Chuck," Lily said to the lettuce. She grabbed it and shut the door.

"Do you have any idea why he's picking on you?" Geeta asked.

"No. I don't even know him. He's in the seventh grade. No one likes him, not even the boys."

"Hmm. Lily…do you think he's bothering you because you're mixed-race?" Geeta was a dark-skinned Indian-American, and Daniel, Lily's father, was white. Lily had her mother's black hair and eyes, and her skin was just dusky enough for her to look "foreign." Geeta was always worried that Lily was going to have a hard time in life because she was mixed-race.

"No! Why should he be? Who cares about race

anyway?" Lily always said that. And usually she didn't care about her skin color. But sometimes she wondered what it would be like not to always have people ask her "where she was from" and have to explain the whole thing.

"Well, then do you think it's because you're so outspoken? You know how you organized that debate—what was it…"

"'Who's Better—Girls or Boys?'" Lily finished her mother's sentence. "I don't know. That was just for my own class. And anyway, it turned out kind of silly. We never came to any conclusion at all, and we just started giggling about half-way through!"

Later, as she sat in bed and tried to read, Lily kept seeing Chuck swaggering towards her with that mocking grin. She imagined what she'd do to him next time he tried anything. She made up cold retorts, and aimed imaginary kicks and stomps.

In her dark bedroom Geeta tossed and turned. She wasn't sure what to do about Chuck. All she could think of doing was calling the principal again. She could call Lauren's mother and talk to her about why Lauren wasn't supporting Lily. But maybe Lauren was right in keeping silent—after all, Lily's fighting back just seemed to goad Chuck on. Should Geeta tell Lily to ignore Chuck?

Not able to come to any conclusion, Geeta fell into a restless sleep.

Chapter 2

What Mrs. Zinn Saw

*L*ily was shoveling in her cereal and milk as fast as she could before her mother finished her shower and came down. She had hidden the box of Choco-Frosted Flakes way in the back of the pasta maker and juicer, still in their boxes, which her parents never had time to use anyway.

But before Lily could consume the last spoonfuls of the forbidden cereal, Geeta dragged herself into the kitchen and sat down heavily at the table. Lily kept eating calmly, hoping her mom wouldn't notice.

"You look tired, Mom."

"I am. I couldn't sleep, trying to figure out what to do about Chuck. D'you think I should call his parents?"

"I don't know. You could try."

"Well, in the meantime, Lily, I want to remind you not to ride your bike too far away from home. Just stick to our own neighborhood. Wait till Dad can go with you on the bike trail. And don't go into those woods! You heard about what happened to those poor girls who took a short-cut through the woods a few months ago."

"But Mom, that happened way out in California. There's a real stream back in the woods! And it even has fish in it, and frogs, and once I saw a heron too!"

"How did you see the heron if you're not allowed to go back there?"

Lily didn't answer, but lifted her bowl to her lips and drank the last of her milk. Then she thought of a good reply. "Mom, you're always saying girls can do anything boys can. If I was a boy, would you let me go there by myself?"

Geeta propped her chin on her hand and looked at Lily wearily. "I don't know. Unfortunately, in our society girls seem to be more in danger than boys. Lily, I don't want to prevent you from having fun. I'm just worried about you, that's all!"

Lily pouted gloomily in the car as Mom drove her to her flute lesson. Mom was always talking about equality and all that—but it didn't seem to apply to her now! It just wasn't fair.

Oh well, she thought. Maybe the lesson would cheer her up. She always enjoyed Mrs. Zinn's company.

Lily knew there was something different about her flute teacher the first time she had a lesson with Mrs. Zinn. It wasn't her house or even her looks that made Lily suspect something. Mrs. Zinn lived in a pretty, sunny old house in the middle of town, with braided rag rugs on the wooden floors, patchwork quilts on the beds, and smells of apples and vanilla. Just like a house should be, thought Lily.

She had her hair colored and done in curls every two weeks. She wore printed turtlenecks and flannel pants and blouses with lace collars. The only thing out of the ordinary were her large eyes—they glowed softly at Lily every time she went in for a lesson. They seemed to see more than other people's eyes.

But what made Lily sure Mrs. Zinn was different was that she knew when Lily hadn't practiced her lesson even before she started playing. And she knew when Lily was hungry or tired—on those days Lily would come in to find tea and cookies waiting for her, and Mrs. Zinn would suggest they skip the lesson and listen to recordings of famous flute players instead.

When Lily told her parents about Mrs. Zinn, they asked, "Couldn't it be that you have a guilty look on your face when you haven't practiced, and that's why Mrs. Zinn can tell? Couldn't it be that since you like tea and cookies almost any time, Mrs. Zinn can't go wrong by offering you some?" Lily could see the point, but wasn't convinced. There was something different about Mrs. Zinn. She just couldn't explain it well enough.

Lily was a little curious about how Mrs. Zinn would react to her mood. She tried to put on a cheerful face, remembering what her parents had said.

"Hello, dear." Mrs. Zinn opened the door onto her neat, warm house. "What awful weather!" she exclaimed with a smile. There were no tea and cookies in sight, and Mrs. Zinn led her straight to the piano room to begin the lesson. As Lily opened her flute case and put the instrument together, she had almost decided her parents were right—that Mrs. Zinn couldn't read minds, but just could read Lily's expressive face like anyone else. She sighed and shuffled her lesson books around to find the right one. As she placed herself in front of the music stand, Mrs. Zinn said,

"It's hard nowadays being a girl."

Lily looked up, surprised, and saw Mrs. Zinn's luminous eyes gazing gently at her. She wanted to ask, "How did you know?" but she found she already had the answer: Mrs. Zinn simply knew.

"Was it easier anytime? Was it easier when you were a girl?" Lily put her flute down and sat in an old armchair covered in a faded fabric.

"When I was a girl it was hard, too." Mrs. Zinn peered at the ceiling from the piano stool where she sat, lost in thought. "I was your age in the 1940s. At that time it was legal to deny a woman a job simply because she was married. I don't know how many talented doctors or musicians we lost because women were home scrubbing floors. Do you know that in many states women could not even serve on juries during a trial?" Mrs. Zinn glared at Lily with outrage.

"I was smart in school," Mrs. Zinn continued. "That wasn't valued in a girl, especially since I didn't hide my pleasure at beating the boys in the spelling bees and other contests we had. And on top of that…" Mrs. Zinn paused…"I saw things. I didn't really know what was happening, only that I saw events just as clearly as if I were there, when I wasn't present at all. At the time one of my brothers was in the army, fighting in Europe. One day in the middle of dinner I stood up and screamed—they say the whole block heard me—but I had seen something horrifying! My brother running, holding his gun, then suddenly the ground shook and he burst into flames. I babbled this to my parents. They were so angry with me for talking about my brother in that way! I was sent to my room. But soon we found out it was true—Bill had been killed by a bomb."

Mrs. Zinn took out a hanky and wiped the corners of her eyes. "I was so shook up by that vision that afterwards I tried to ignore the things I saw. I didn't talk about them to anyone. If I'd trusted myself more, I probably could've helped my family and friends avoid bad decisions and accidents." Mrs. Zinn's voice lowered almost to a whisper. "I count that as my biggest failure—not trying to help people with my gift of sight."

Mrs. Zinn sat staring at the piano keys. Lily said softly, "But maybe people wouldn't have believed you if you tried to give them advice."

"You're right, they probably wouldn't have, especially since I was just a young girl. But I know of a time when girls did stop disasters, because they had my gift, and important people listened to them. It was a time when women were considered just as important as men—maybe even a little more important."

"When was that?" Lily tucked her legs under her and riveted her eyes on Mrs. Zinn's face in eager expectation of the story.

But Mrs. Zinn became suddenly brisk. "No

more of that now. It's time for your lesson. That's what your parents pay for, after all." She stood up to adjust the music stand to Lily's height.

Lily was not about to play etudes now. She tried to distract Mrs. Zinn by thinking hard of how hungry she was for cookies. When Mrs. Zinn did nothing but play a scale on the piano, Lily said, "Couldn't we have something to eat before we start?"

Mrs. Zinn looked at her and laughed. "You're right. I've made you too curious now, and it's not fair not to tell you the rest. Tell your parents I won't charge for this lesson. What kind of cookies would you like—lemon or pecan?"

Chapter 3

Dinosaurs and Priestesses

*L*ily and Mrs. Zinn settled into huge overstuffed armchairs in the living room, with mint tea and cookies. "What I'm going to tell you happened a long time ago," began Mrs. Zinn. "About 3,500 years ago."

Lily was hesitant to reveal her ignorance, but she had to ask. "But—were there even humans at that time?"

"Modern humans have existed for about 200,000 years."

Lily could hardly imagine that many years. "Then we must have been around when the dinosaurs were!"

"Oh no, of course not! Dinosaurs were around hundreds of millions of years ago! The earth itself was probably formed almost five billion years ago. So really, 3,500 years ago is quite recent when you think about how old the earth is, and how long life has been on it. Anyhow, in our recent past, there lived a girl named Phyra on an island

named Crete." Lily noticed Mrs. Zinn was holding what looked like a green coin in one hand as she spoke. It had been carved prettily all over.

"Phyra lived with her mother, grandmother, father, sisters and brothers, aunts and uncles, cousins—" Mrs. Zinn stopped. "You think the house must have been crowded, don't you? Well, it wasn't because they had many little houses connected with porches and passageways. Phyra had a wonderful childhood playing in the meadows in the town, with other children and the birds, chipmunks, insects, and flowers. She also helped her mother in the garden, and learned to dye and weave cloth from flax and hemp. There were no schools then." Mrs. Zinn paused to sip her tea slowly. "Phyra learned what she wanted from whichever adults could teach her, and from observing people and nature. There weren't any books at that time, either.

"But what Phyra enjoyed most was going to the palace with her family on every full moon to hear the prophesies of the Queen-priestess. The Queen-priestess wore a full, layered, colorful skirt which she had dyed and sewn herself. She lived in the palace with her husband and children and many other priestesses and priests. Phyra loved to hear her sing the prophecies every month, and she loved the rare occasions when the Queen came to her family's house for dinner. Then they all played games and the Queen told stories for the children just before bedtime. Phyra thought she wanted to be a palace priestess someday."

Mrs. Zinn glanced at Lily. "How are you doing with your tea? Do you find this story very strange?"

"Things certainly were different then, even if it wasn't so long ago. What happened next? Did Phyra become a priestess?"

"Listen, and you'll see. Phyra's mother and grandmother were weavers and dyers, and they were training Phyra in those arts. Back then children followed the profession of their mothers, instead of choosing their own the way we do now. So her family tried to discourage her from becoming a priestess. But Phyra felt so strongly it was her calling to be a priestess that finally, her family agreed.

"After Phyra got her period and was old enough to train as a priestess, she went to the palace to live. Her parents were a little nervous, because training as a priestess was difficult. Many young women and men quit, and were discouraged and depressed. Phyra spent long hours chanting, meditating, and doing rituals of one kind and another, in order to awaken her psychic powers, if she had them. She felt calm and happy during this time, and often thought she saw visions of the Goddess in her many forms—birds, bees, snakes, bulls, and a large woman with babies.

"One day she saw a vision that the town would experience a powerful earthquake, more powerful than had occurred in many decades. Other priestesses also had similar visions, and they told the Queen, who recommended elaborate rituals, including the sacrificing of animals, to appease the spirits who lived in the soil. 'They may be jealous since we've been living so well for so many years,' explained the Queen. Phyra had seen the storerooms in the palace, with rows and rows of huge clay urns filled with olives, cheese in salted water, pickled fish, wine, and oil. The food was distributed to the people every time the seasons changed.

"Everyone in town was worried, and spent their days wondering whether their own precious pottery, or their houses, would be destroyed in the earthquake. Many people decided to try to hold onto as many of their possessions as possible during the quake, to prevent them from being broken. Others said this was a silly and

perhaps even dangerous practice: if the soil spirits were indeed jealous, they may cause more harm
to befall those who held fast to their wealth.

"The rituals, sacrifices and worrying went on.
The day before the earthquake was to occur, Phyra
had another vision. She saw a pretty blue bird in
the meadow. It said, 'I am the sky. Come out and
play with me, and I will save you.' Phyra again
told her vision to the Queen, who decided sacrifices and prayers were in order for the sky-spirits
as well, so they would help the townspeople.

"But Phyra disagreed. 'We should do exactly
as the bird says—leave our homes and go play
under the sky.' Perhaps Phyra felt this way because it had been months since she'd played freely
in the meadow. She'd been so busy with her work
inside the palace she'd almost forgotten about the
simple joy she felt watching the ants at work, or
looking for the sweet red berries that hid under
fuzzy, prickly green leaves.

"The Queen hesitated for a moment. Phyra's
suggestion seemed a little uncivilized to her. But
she remembered stories she'd heard from her
grandmother—how long ago the people of the
town prayed simply by going outside and looking, seeing, smelling, and touching the plants and
living creatures. The Queen also remembered an

old saying: 'Let youths lead elders on new paths.'

"So the townspeople did just as Phyra recommended. They went outside to wait for the earthquake, which arrived just as predicted. Children and many adults were crying and praying with fright. People held onto tall weeds or clutched at grasses as the ground shook under them. After several minutes it was over, and no one was hurt since they were out in the open where nothing could fall on them. Some food and pottery was lost, but the people had so much they could afford to lose a little."

Mrs. Zinn sank back in her chair. Lily was still leaning forward, her eyes fixed on Mrs. Zinn's face. She couldn't let Mrs. Zinn rest yet—she had to know more.

"What happened to Phyra after that?" she asked insistently.

Mrs. Zinn's eyes looked deep and sad. The big hand on the mantle clock creaked forward. Finally Mrs. Zinn said,

"Some years after that earthquake, Crete experienced a massive flood and invasions by surrounding people who were not as peaceful or willing to share as the Cretans were. I don't know what happened to Phyra, but I do know that Cretan society was never the same again. Warriors took over the palace, keeping the best food and treasures for themselves. The palace was abandoned. Cretan families were torn apart, and the boys trained to be soldiers, the girls to be maids for the conquerors."

"How did you know about Phyra?" asked Lily. "Is it written down?"

"Few historical records have come down to us from that time." Mrs. Zinn's eyes seemed to be glowing, penetrating the walls of the house. "I know because I've been there." She put the green "coin" she had been holding on the coffee table. It seemed almost to float above the table for a few minutes, shimmering in a light both faint and illuminating. But when Lily reached out to pick it up, it became just a small stone disk in her hands. It felt very warm.

Chapter 4

The Necklace of Time

*L*ily looked at Mrs. Zinn. Telling the story about Phyra seemed to have tired her out, and she looked almost like a child about to fall asleep. After a few minutes Lily asked softly, "How did you get to where Phyra was?"

Mrs. Zinn opened her eyes and sat up straight. She looked hard at Lily for one full minute. Lily looked back boldly, right into her eyes.

"Yes, I think I can tell you," said Mrs. Zinn finally, almost to herself. She plumped up the pillow she was leaning against and slipped it behind her again, placing her hands neatly in her lap. "There are many ways to travel in time. But most important to any method is this: you must suspend your belief in time. You must not think of events as happening in the past or future. You must not even think of them as happening in the present!"

"When do they happen, then?"

"'When' is not a word you can use without

time, is it? Some people say all years, months, days, and seconds, are all in the mind of a Universal Being—what Phyra called the Goddess. Others say the years are like a string of beads—you thread the beads one at a time, but they're all there before you make the necklace, and they're still there after it breaks. The events that take place in those years, however—that depends on what we decide to do."

Lily nodded solemnly, trying not to look too confused. She rubbed the green disk absent-mindedly. Mrs. Zinn took it from her and held it up.

"This seal is from Crete. I got it from an archeologist friend. It's my ticket to that place and time. Once I've managed to suspend my belief in time (no easy task, let me tell you), I hold an object from where I want to go and ask it to take me there. The technique itself is quite simple. You don't need any fancy computers or machines, like they show in the movies."

Lily's heart was racing with excitement. If it was that simple, she wanted to travel in time too! "Can you teach me how?" she asked breathlessly, her eyes sparkling.

Mrs. Zinn looked at her and laughed. "You're almost jumping out of your skin!" she exclaimed.

"I might be able to teach you, but only if you have the talent. Even then I'm not sure it would work. I've never tried to teach time-travel to anyone before."

"Oh, please try now!" pleaded Lily. "I promise I'll practice every day—even for an hour, if I have to."

Mrs. Zinn smiled. "Well, first you should be sure you like time-travel. Would you like to go on a trip with me soon?"

Lily shouted happily. "Yes, yes, YES!! When do we leave? Do I have to pack my toothbrush?"

"What you bring depends on where and to what time we go. Where would you like to go? It's just as easy—or hard—to go back to the beginning of time as it is to go back to yesterday—if we have an object from that time period, that is."

"What's the earliest time you have an object for?"

"Well…" Mrs. Zinn put her finger to her lips in thought. "I've never really concentrated on gathering objects for time-travel. I think I have a little fossil of a trilobite." She opened a drawer of a little wooden side table. Lily saw a tangle of rubber bands, string, marbles, and paper clips. Mrs. Zinn rummaged around and produced a dime-sized piece of gray stone. It looked like a cross between a beetle and a centipede. Lily would have been delighted to catch something like that and put it in a jar to watch.

"Trilobites are one of Earth's first animals, and they lived in shallow seas," Mrs. Zinn explained as Lily rubbed the smooth stone belly of the creature. "In fact, everything lived in the seas back then—there was no life on land. If we were to go back I imagine it would be dull, since we can't go into the ocean where the action was. I think the weather was hot and humid in many places, and of course there were no trees to cool things off— just rocks and mountains and volcanoes. I'm not sure I'd trust myself to go back that far. There's always the possibility I'll be hurt or get sick and won't be able to create the proper state of mind to come back. And then where would we be, with no other people and only seafood to eat?"

Lily agreed that trilobite time wouldn't be the best time to go back to. "What other old objects do you have?"

"Besides this seal from Crete, I might have some jewelry from my great-grandmother, dating to the beginning of this century."

The beginning of the century didn't seem nearly long enough ago to be interesting. Lily picked up the green seal again. "I wonder... should we go back and see what happened to Phyra? Maybe we can even help her since we know what happens later!"

"Now, Lily, that's the one thing that I'll ask you not to do," said Mrs. Zinn sternly. "If I take you back in time with me, you must promise not to try to do anything grand and heroic to save someone's life or prevent a disaster. You must not even tell anyone about the flood and invasions I told you about. It may seem like a good idea to you, but you can't tell what the consequences down the road might be. Why, if we prevent this invasion of Crete, perhaps a more violent culture (although that's hard to imagine) would have invaded them some years down the line. For example, many years ago a very kindhearted friend of mine went back to 18th-century France because she was fascinated by the French Revolution, and—well, to make a long story short she saved the life of a little boy who would have otherwise died. This boy grew up, married, had many children, and as it turns out one of his descendants was the man who designed the first bikini, of all things! It was very scandalous in my time, but now it's every woman's dream to be as thin as a rail so she can wear a bikini. I tell my friend every time we meet that she's quite responsible for all the diet fads nowadays. Of course she feels badly, but she says she couldn't let the poor boy die when she, being a nurse, knew exactly how to cure him. So there you have it, Lily, and let that be a lesson to you."

Lily was already thinking about when she would be able leave to go to Crete. Thanksgiving was pretty soon, but she was sure her parents would expect her to be at home for that. "Won't my parents be worried if we stay away too long?" Lily asked.

"The convenient thing about time-travel is that it takes no time at all in the present. We can go and return and still have time for your lesson!" Mrs. Zinn looked pleased. Lily was sure she wouldn't want a flute lesson after being in Crete! After some discussion, they decided to go back to Crete the next week, during Lily's flute lesson.

Lily packed up her flute quickly and opened the door. Sometimes Mrs. Zinn talked a little too much! Mrs. Zinn laid a hand on Lily's arm.

"One last thing, Lily. You must not tell anyone that you're a time-traveler. Because time-travel can change history, those of us who do it pledge not to broadcast the information. And you must pledge so too."

"Okay," Lily said, too excited to think about such details.

"And Lily," Mrs. Zinn continued, "you must try your best not to get hurt or sick in Crete. Because if something were to happen to you—if you were to die—it would be as if you'd never existed in present time!"

Lily ran out the door. "Don't worry, Mrs. Zinn. I'll do everything you say!" And she jumped into the waiting car.

Chapter 5

The Trip

*L*ily could hardly keep her plans to herself all week. She was so distracted she forgot completely about a book report that was due Wednesday, and had to write it feverishly during lunch. Fortunately, Chuck was nowhere to be seen the whole week.

Finally, Saturday arrived. She took a shower, slipped a skirt into her backpack (in Crete no one wore jeans), and bounded down the stairs. "I'm ready, Dad!" she yelled.

Geeta and Daniel were sitting at the kitchen table with the newspaper spread out all over, nibbling dried peaches and sipping hot ginseng tea.

"Aren't you going to eat anything, Lily?" her dad asked. "I just made some cherry-almond granola."

Lily was too excited to eat. "Mrs. Zinn said I had to get to her house early today." She grabbed the car keys from their hook and started toward the door. "I'll be waiting in the car."

"Lily," her mom said, "aren't you forgetting something?"

Lily turned around and mentally checked off the items in her backpack. Skirt, lucky arrowhead she'd found on the playground, a paperback book called *The Mystery of the Cauldron*. "No," she said.

"What about your flute?"

"Oh, yeah!" Lily took the stairs two at a time, grabbed her instrument, and ran down again, jumping off the next-to-last step.

As they drove to Mrs. Zinn's house, Dad asked, "So what're you so excited about today? Is Mrs. Zinn planning a recital?"

"No." Lily tried to look a little less excited so Dad wouldn't get too suspicious.

"Is it a contest? Are you getting ready for that contest that happens every year?"

"No. Aren't the leaves pretty now?" She knew this would distract her dad, since he really liked talking about red and yellow fall leaves.

"They sure are! When I was coming back from Arizona I could see all the beautiful red trees from the plane! It was absolutely breathtaking!"

They pulled up in front of Mrs. Zinn's house. Lily flung the car door open and scrambled out.

"I'll be back in an hour," Dad called as she ran toward the house.

Mrs. Zinn greeted her at the door in a flowing long skirt and short blouse. "I picked this up last time I was in ancient Crete," Mrs. Zinn explained, as though she were talking about a trip to Europe. "Actually, most of the time the women don't even wear blouses, but I'm not used to that kind of thing. Now—have you brought your skirt? We'll get you into some real Cretan clothes once we get there. We'll be staying with a dear friend of mine, whose daughter is about the same age as you are. Go put your skirt on—we may as well get started."

Lily hadn't realized they were going to be staying overnight. "How long will we be there for?"

"Oh…it will seem like a few weeks, or even longer, but of course it won't be any time at all. I have a few things I'd like to do there. I was planning to go anyway."

Lily's excitement started to turn into nervousness. She went into the bathroom to change. But once the door was closed, instead of putting on her clothing she sat down on the toilet seat cover. A few weeks! Or longer! Even if it wasn't any time at all, as Mrs. Zinn insisted, it would still seem like a long time to be far away from home. Should she decide not to go after all?

Lily looked around at the neat bathroom, with

matching peach-colored towels, rug, shower curtain, even peach-colored little soaps shaped like shells. If she stayed home, how boring life would be, especially after discovering this secret about Mrs. Zinn hiding behind her commonplace house and looks. She wanted to go, even if she was scared a little. She jumped up, pulled off her jeans, and buttoned on her skirt and blouse.

"Mrs. Zinn!" she called as she opened the door. "Can I ask you a question?"

"Certainly, dear." Mrs. Zinn was sitting calmly in the living room, knitting what looked like a baby sweater out of a skein of pale pink yarn. "My son's wife is going to have a baby! A little girl," Mrs. Zinn smiled happily. "They haven't told me yet, but since I saw the child already I thought I might as well start on a few things for it. What did you want to ask me?"

"Well...if we get to Crete and I don't like it ...I mean, I'm sure I will, but if I don't...do you think we could come home sooner than a few weeks?"

Mrs. Zinn laid her knitting in her lap and sat silently in thought several seconds. "Well, as I mentioned I was hoping to be there long enough to do a few things. If you fell ill, I would of course bring you home immediately. But if it were just homesickness—do you get homesick easily? Because if you do, maybe we should wait for a shorter trip for you to go with me."

Lily couldn't think of waiting. "I don't think I've ever gotten homesick, and I've stayed with my grandparents lots of times by myself. I'm sure I'll be fine." She smiled bravely. Her head was swimming and her heart beat rapidly.

"Fabulous," said Mrs. Zinn. "Then we'll start." She turned off the radio, which had been playing classical music, pulled down the blinds, and settled back into her chair. She was holding the green seal in her hand. "Sit right here next to me and hold my hand, Lily. Now close your eyes, breathe deeply, and try to make your mind blank." It sounded just like Dad when he was trying to get Lily to meditate.

They sat in silence for a few minutes. The more Lily tried to make her mind blank, the more her thoughts wandered. She thought about the story Mrs. Zinn told about Crete, and about the field trip her class was taking the next week, and about how Mom said they were having pizza for dinner. Her nose itched, and the waistband of her skirt felt too tight. She even opened her eyes for a second and looked over at Mrs. Zinn. Her eyes were closed and she looked like she was asleep, except Lily knew she wasn't from the tight grip she kept on Lily's hand. Then—

Lily couldn't describe how she was feeling—kind of like she had no body anymore. She couldn't see or hear or feel anything, but still she somehow felt like she was being sucked or propelled through something very fast. She couldn't tell how long it lasted. It wasn't painful, but it didn't feel good either, and Lily couldn't wait to be done with it and be together again in one place.

Suddenly she could see, hear, and feel again. She and Mrs. Zinn were sitting on a beach, still holding hands. Mrs. Zinn laughed delightedly. "I did it! We're here!"

Lily looked around in amazement and a little fear. The sky was a clear blue, and the sea sparkled with golden flecks of sunlight. The sand they were sitting on was pleasantly warm. It looked so normal Lily wondered whether Mrs. Zinn hadn't transported them to California by mistake. Then she saw two people walking down the beach. They were both wearing very short skirts, and both had long dark hair flowing over their shoulders. Lily had never seen clothes like that before. To Lily's surprise and embarrassment, they stripped off their skirts to reveal no clothes underneath, and she saw that one was a young man and one a young woman. They both ran laughing into the waves.

"Yes, I should have warned you that here in Crete, no one is very worried about clothing—they'd sooner have it off than on!" Mrs. Zinn laughed again and stood up to brush off her skirt. "Well, we may as well make our way to my friend Inasha's house." She started walking, and Lily jumped up to follow her.

Chapter 6

The Town

*T*he path they followed took them past the harbor, where men and women with their hair tied up were lifting heavy bags and baskets out of long rowboats with three or four sets of oars. Lily saw a few ships with folded sails farther out at sea. In the direction they were walking, the island was thickly wooded in the distance.

They were now walking uphill, among neat orchards and past clusters of houses. A cart drawn by an ox rumbled past them on the wide road. Lily saw people working in gardens, strumming instruments and singing, and playing with children. It was hard to tell if they were men or women sometimes because all wore their hair long, and many had on short skirts. Many of them looked at Lily and Mrs. Zinn and waved.

"Don't they think it's strange to see us here?" asked Lily, surprised that people didn't stare at her.

"They're used to visitors. People are always

sailing in from the lands we call Greece, Egypt, Turkey, the Middle East, and even England. But you can be sure they'll find out who we are. With no TV or radio or movies, people here spend a lot of time gossiping!" Mrs. Zinn laughed.

Lily was getting tired and hungry. She was starting to regret not eating the granola Dad made. She saw they were walking past a pear orchard, where the fruit was hanging ripe and rosy. "I wish I could eat one of those!" she exclaimed.

"Go ahead. You don't even have to wash it because they haven't invented pesticides yet. Watch out for worms, though!"

"But won't we get into trouble? Don't these trees belong to someone?"

"They belong to everyone. The garden beside each house belongs to the family that lives in that house. But the orchards and the wheat fields are for everyone. The rule is that you may eat a few pears or figs if you're hungry, but you must not take a basket of them home without letting the caretaker know. Each family is allotted a certain portion."

Lily reached up and plucked a pear. She inspected it for worm holes and, finding none, took a big, juicy, sweet bite.

Soon they reached Mrs. Zinn's friend's house.

It looked a lot like all the other houses. They all seemed to have lots of shaded porches, and clusters of buildings grouped together any which way. It was hard to figure out where the entrance was. Outside the house a gray-haired man was sitting and shelling peas. Mrs. Zinn walked up to him, sat down, and started talking in a strange language. He looked at her and smiled, taking both her hands in his own. Then he smiled at Lily and patted the bench beside him. Lily hurried to sit down, since he seemed so eager to make her comfortable.

The man and Mrs. Zinn talked for what seemed like several minutes (Lily couldn't be sure because her watch had suddenly stopped). At one point he looked at Lily and asked a question. Mrs. Zinn said something which must have answered the question, because he looked at Lily again and nodded.

Finally Mrs. Zinn got up. "Come on. Let's get you some proper clothes." She walked into the house and Lily followed. "That was Inasha's father," she said as they made their way through the dim, cool house. "He asked me where you're from, and I told him you're from what we call Lebanon. That seemed to make sense since your hair and skin are darker than a European's, which is what I'm claiming to be.

"Inasha's at the pottery workshop," Mrs. Zinn continued. "She's one of the best potters in Crete." Mrs. Zinn opened wooden cabinet doors in the storeroom and collected a long skirt and blouse for Lily. "Try these on."

The skirt was simple, with a v-shaped pattern in light blue on a yellow background. Lily tied it around her waist and slipped the yellow blouse over her head.

"You'd better take your watch off," Mrs. Zinn said. "That would make people suspicious." Lily gave her watch to Mrs. Zinn, who put it in a small wooden box and hid it in the back of the cabinet.

"Now for sandals," Mrs. Zinn muttered as she crawled around the floor, searching the low shelves of the cabinets. She drew out a pair of leather sandals with thick straps. Lily sat down on a bench to fasten them with their substantial gold-colored buckles.

When she looked up she saw Mrs. Zinn sitting on a bench gazing around, deep in thought. The walls of this room were covered with cabinets, and even the benches they were sitting on opened so you could store things in them.

"What do you think of Crete so far?" Mrs. Zinn broke the silence.

Lily thought for a moment. "It seems so—modern! All these buildings and ships and...I thought you said we were going back in time a long way!"

Mrs. Zinn laughed. "Our culture owes a lot to the Cretans. Did you know the potter's wheel was invented on this island? And it's my feeling that our American democracy would not be even as fair and equal as it is, if Crete hadn't influenced Greek democracy.

"Now," Mrs. Zinn got up, "let's go see Inasha and let her know we're here.

Chapter 7

The Palace

*T*he pottery workshop was inside the palace. As they walked up the slope, Lily saw the palace's facade come into focus out of the fields where cows and sheep were grazing. At several places, what looked like horns seemed to be protruding from the palace roof. "Those are sculptures of bull's horns," explained Mrs. Zinn. "The bull is a sacred animal for the Cretans." The palace was certainly large, but it had no towers and it didn't look very grand or imposing, the way Lily imagined a palace would be. In fact, it looked kind of funny with its horns sticking up like that.

Lily saw people sitting on the porch, talking and laughing. As they got closer Lily noticed that both the men and women wore make-up to darken the outlines of their eyes and redden their lips. Both wore jewelry and gold or silver belts. They both left their chests bare.

"Those people are the queen's helpers," Mrs. Zinn whispered. "They lead quite a comfortable

life, I must say. Every time I see them they're talking, or eating, or singing, or playing games. They must find time to do their work, though, since the taxes get paid and the festivals and banquets never fail to take place."

Mrs. Zinn led Lily through hallways and rooms, and up and down stairs. Lily tried to remember the route they were taking, but she turned so many corners she couldn't keep it straight. Finally they came to the workshop, a large, airy, light-filled room. Lily gazed in silence at the dozen or more potters deftly forming vases, bowls, plates, cups, and other objects, which took shape under their fingers as the potter's wheels whirled. Several more people sat at desks by the windows, painting the formed and hardened pieces. Lily stepped quietly over to a painter and watched as the outlines of an octopus appeared on a pitcher, its eight long legs curled around the pitcher's round shape.

Mrs. Zinn had found Inasha, and was now hugging her. They were both laughing and talking at the same time. Lily walked around the studio and watched other potters and painters. She especially liked one plate showing a monkey trying to catch butterflies, which were so colorful and vibrant they seemed almost ready to fly off the plate!

Mrs. Zinn sure was talking to Inasha for a long time. Lily was bored with the lack of activity. She saw a hallway near the bench she was sitting on. Should she explore? She looked at Mrs. Zinn, who showed no intention of getting up to leave. Lily stood up and ducked into the passageway.

It was dim, but she saw light ahead. She wandered down the hall, through a doorway, and into another hall. She heard voices, and followed the sounds into a large room with pillars.

Groups of women and men sat on soft stools, or on the floor. One little toddler was crying on a man's lap. The man rocked the baby back and forth to soothe it. Children ran around, and a few played some kind of board game. The walls and pillars were painted with colorful abstract waves and spirals and flowers. Daylight brightened the room through a few skylights.

A woman nursing her baby near the doorway noticed Lily and placed her hand on the center of her chest, seemingly in greeting. Lily smiled hesitantly and made the same gesture. She stood at the door for a few minutes, not sure whether it was OK to enter. But no one seemed upset she was there, so she walked in to look at the game the children were playing. The game board was inlaid with intricate designs made of colored stones and metal—blue, pink, white, black and gold. It was so beautiful it belonged in a museum, Lily thought.

She looked hard at the two players to decide if they were girls or boys. Both had long hair and flat chests, and were wearing short skirts. She couldn't decide what they were. It felt strange not knowing whether they were boys or girls, or one of each.

The game was proceeding very slowly. It seemed to require a lot of thought, after which one of the players would move a disk one space. Lily yawned and looked around. Maybe she should go back to Mrs. Zinn.

Just then a little kid ran by, pulled Lily's hair, and ran away squealing. She saw a group of small children giggling at her. She looked down at herself. Was she wearing something strange? She must look out of place somehow, despite the borrowed clothes.

The same kid came back and tugged at her arm, saying something and motioning her to come. She got up to follow. Maybe they just wanted a playmate!

They ran out a door, through a few more rooms, down a long hallway, and outside into the bright sunshine. Lily squinted and blinked. She hadn't realized how dim it was inside the palace. They raced around on the scrubby grass. Lily laughed and chased the kid who'd pulled her hair, and picked up a toddler who'd fallen down. Other children were rolling down the little hills and dips around the palace.

Lily sat down on a warm rock to catch her breath. The children ran out of sight around the corner of the palace. Lily could see down from the palace hill, across fields and houses to the ocean. She heard sheep bleating and a few distant shouts. Every so often a gentle breeze fluttered her skirt.

She was very hungry. She ought to find Mrs. Zinn and see about getting supper. She started to walk back towards the palace. In their race to get outdoors, Lily hadn't paid attention to the path they took. She knew she was going in by a different door, but how hard could it be to find the pottery workshop again?

She entered a shaded porch and gazed with interest at a painting covering one wall. A bull was stretched out in midair, and a man painted red was balancing on its back by his hands. The man was smiling, and Lily thought it looked like he had a pretty silly grin on his face considering his dangerous feat. Lily wondered if they had a circus in Crete, and if this was a painting of it.

Then Lily walked down a hallway lined with more paintings: two rows, one above the other, of life-sized figures of women and men carrying things—gifts, maybe. They were also all smiling. She was glad the Cretans were so cheerful, at least in their paintings.

At the end of the corridor she turned left and continued. Several doorways on the right opened onto a long terrace where people were lounging and eating. She looked at their fruits and bread and cheese longingly. But they didn't see her or offer her food, so she walked on.

There were some dark corridors on the left. She wasn't sure whether she should turn into one of them. She was kind of afraid of the dark. She stopped at one to see if she could hear any sign of the pottery workshop. But she heard nothing. She didn't know where to turn, and she couldn't even ask the people on the terrace where the pottery workshop was. She'd have to get Mrs. Zinn to teach her a few words fast.

She listened carefully for voices to guide her back. Finally she heard some in the distance, and followed them. As they grew louder, she realized they were chanting or singing.

Chapter 8

The Ceremony

*L*ily walked to the end of the hallway and found herself in a large courtyard open to the sky. It was bigger than their gym at school. She saw doorways and staircases in the walls, and two tiers of balconies held up with red columns. Colorful spirals, circles, and flowers adorned the walls and decorated the edges of the doorways. It was beautiful! Lily was sure she hadn't been through this courtyard before. Should she turn back and try another route?

Since she was here already, she thought she might as well explore a little bit. She looked around to see if anyone was watching her, and she saw no one.

She edged into the courtyard and walked softly right next to the wall, gazing around her. Black birds flew across the blue sky above her. Low-growing herbs and tiny flowers crept out among the flagstones on the ground.

The chanting was coming through a doorway farther along the wall. When she got there, she peeked in and saw wide, low steps leading into an empty room. Benches lined the walls, which were painted with bulls and flowers and strange animals she'd never seen before. The singing seemed to be coming from behind the curtains at the opposite end of the room.

Should she go in further? She looked over her shoulder and still saw no one watching her, so she quickly stepped into the room. She tiptoed across the floor and put one eye up to a space between the curtains. The voices were quite loud now, but still she saw no one.

The room into which she looked was brightly painted and pretty. Again, Lily saw strange creatures painted on the walls on a background of broad, wavy bands of red and white. What looked like little bamboo plants were also painted on the walls. The animals looked like lions with birds' heads. Lily wondered whether these animals were real—had they traveled back far enough in time for such things to exist? But she'd never seen a skeleton of an animal like that at the museum.

Against one wall stood a raised, high-backed chair with no arm rests, painted pink. Its back had a wavy edge, and looked like an oak leaf from the big tree in their backyard. Could this be where the queen sat? Was that her throne? But the room didn't look anything like the grand, high-ceilinged throne rooms she'd seen in pictures of palaces from Europe and India. It was so small, and looked almost like a play room for children.

On the left, behind three columns and enclosed by low walls, was what looked like a tiny swimming pool. A few stairs led down to the level of the water. Lily was hot after running around outside. She took off her sandals, went down the stairs, and started wading in the water. She felt little touches on her ankles, and looking down, saw that there were goldfish in the water! Their plump orange bodies glowed as they glided and flicked back and forth among waving green plants. She watched them, mesmerized, for a few minutes.

The singing grew suddenly louder, and she hastened back up the stairs, feet dripping, and put her sandals on. She hoped she wouldn't get in trouble for leaving wet footprints!

There was another doorway at the end of the room. She stepped softly across the floor, and peeked into the next room.

It was dark, except for a tall lamp burning in the corner. Five or six women stood with their backs to Lily, singing. Lily wasn't sure it was all right for her to be watching, and started to edge away from the doorway. Just then a woman with graying hair glanced at her. The woman's large brown eyes glowed at Lily in the dim lamplight. She beckoned Lily to come in, and made a space for her in the semicircle.

Lily hesitated. What was she getting herself into? What would they expect her to do? Would they discover she wasn't a Cretan and punish her for intruding on their ceremony? Before Lily could decide what to do, the woman reached out, took Lily's hand, and pulled her gently forward into the space.

Lily's eyes grew adjusted to the darkness, and she saw statues on the ledge in front of her, statues of women dressed in the same layered dresses these women were wearing. These goddesses seemed to be holding snakes in their upraised hands, or letting snakes crawl on them. But they didn't look alarmed at all. In fact, they were smiling brightly with their eyes open wide. Surrounding the idols were fruits, flowers, and shells.

Lily thought it was a lot like the Indian ceremonies she'd seen her grandmother perform. She started to relax a little, and hoped the ceremony wouldn't take too long. Her grandmother's always seemed to last forever! A woman handed her a flask and motioned for her to pour a little of its contents into a bowl. Lily did so—it seemed to be oil, and it smelled like perfume.

After all the women had poured some oil, they stopped singing. That was the end of the ceremony, and as they filed out of the room they talked and laughed with each other. The woman who'd pulled Lily in asked her a question.

"I don't understand!" Lily said, trying to smile as politely as she could. She needed to get back to Mrs. Zinn and Inasha, but how could she get directions from these women?

They sat on low chairs in the courtyard, and someone handed Lily some almonds and grapes. She almost forgot she was lost in her delight at getting something to eat! The sweet juiciness of the grapes, and the smooth, woody almonds sent waves of bliss over her.

After she'd satisfied her hunger, she turned to the gray-haired woman and said, "Where is the pottery workshop?" She made the shapes of a vase and a plate in the air with her hands.

But the woman just looked at her with a puzzled expression. Then Lily thought the woman might know Inasha's name. "Inasha. I want to go where Inasha is."

The woman repeated, "Inasha?", then started talking to the woman beside her, pointing to Lily. The second woman asked Lily a question, enunciating each word very slowly. Lily still didn't understand, of course. She looked around the courtyard for some kind of prop or clue, and she saw two children drawing on the paving stones with chalk. She ran over to them and held out her hand for a piece of chalk, which they gave her. Then she ran back to the two women and started drawing on the ground the vase with the octopus she'd seen.

"Aah! Inasha!" And the women started talking to each other rapidly. They stood up and led her out the courtyard and back into the maze of hallways and rooms. Soon she was back in the pottery workshop. Their entrance seemed to cause a commotion. The potters exclaimed and all got up to greet the women.

Mrs. Zinn took Lily aside, scolded her for walking off by herself, and informed her sternly that she could have been lost for days—the palace was a very confusing place—she could have gotten into the storerooms and never been seen or heard from for weeks, even! Lily nodded, but couldn't believe she'd been in any danger. And if she had, well, it was a better story to tell her friends when she got home! But she had to admit she was very relieved to finally be reunited with Mrs. Zinn.

Chapter 9

Evening

As they walked back to Inasha's house, Mrs. Zinn explained the things Lily had seen in the palace. The first room Lily had come to, the one with the children playing the board game, was a kind of lounge area for people who worked in the palace. The children of the palace workers could spend time there if they wanted.

The rooms off the courtyard, where the ceremony had taken place, were the queen's throne rooms. Lily had witnessed the daily prayers of the palace priestesses. In fact, the woman who had drawn Lily into the ceremony was the Queen herself! And the second woman who'd led Lily back was Phyra, the head priestess, whose story Mrs. Zinn had told Lily.

"But in the future, Lily, try not to attract the attention of the Queen, or the priestesses, for that matter. If they start wondering too much about where we're from or what we're doing here, they might decide we're a bad omen, and who knows what would happen then?"

"Would they lock us up in those storerooms?" Lily thought about what might be lurking in all the dark nooks and corners of the palace.

"No. They'd probably just tell us never to come back. That would be bad enough, though, since I have such good friends here."

Supper was ready for them at home. Inasha's father and mother had made it. They all sat on the porch, because it was such a nice evening. There were about a dozen people. Lily later learned the others were Inasha's sisters and their families.

Lily met Inasha's daughter, whose name was Mashi. She had curly hair and a friendly smile. Her feet were dirty, and she had a fat tummy that stuck out over her short skirt. Lily felt embarrassed for her because she looked sort of slobby. But Mashi wasn't shy or self-conscious at all. She sat down beside Lily on the porch steps and started pointing to Lily's plate and saying words. Lily guessed she was trying to teach her the language, so she repeated what Mashi said.

The food wasn't that great, but Lily did her best to eat it, since she didn't have much choice. They had some cold meat, brown bread, some sour, salty yogurt with raw peas, and carrots with herbs. For dessert they each got a piece of honey-comb. Mashi was ecstatic! Lily thought with relief that squash hadn't yet been brought to this part of the world—no more squash soup for a while, at least. But Mrs. Zinn had told her there was no chocolate, or melons, or corn-on-the-cob, either. It was amazing to realize that none of these foods were known to Cretans! They grew only in what we call North America, planted and tended by the tribes.

After supper everyone brought out some hobby or game onto the porch. Inasha's husband Edani was a carpenter, and he was carving some wood in his spare time. It was going to be a stool for a woman to sit on when she was having a baby. He said something about it to Mashi, who retorted something back, and everyone laughed. Mrs. Zinn leaned over and told Lily that Edani was pretending the stool was for Mashi, and that he was waiting for her to get pregnant so he could stop working on it. Mashi told him he was so slow she'd have to have all her children on the ground. Lily couldn't imagine joking with her father about getting pregnant. Whenever he talked about things like that he always got real serious and quiet and used the word "responsible" a lot.

Lily was so tired she could barely keep her eyes open, and soon fell asleep on the porch.

Chapter 10

Looking Good

*L*ily rubbed her eyes. She was lying on the floor, and sunlight was slanting into a little room. She looked around and saw Mrs. Zinn on one side of her, and Mashi on the other side. It took her a minute to remember where she was. Then she realized—she was in the middle of an adventure!

After breakfast (which was something like thick oatmeal), she, Mashi, and Mrs. Zinn set off for the palace. Mashi was being trained as a potter, just like her mother and grandmother, and Lily was to go along and learn a few basics.

A golden sun warmed them as they walked under a blue sky. Lily was still a little hungry and tired. Mashi was very excited about something. Mrs. Zinn translated for Lily. "They're having a contest for the Autumn Festival, and Mashi and her friend are going to make a sculpture of a bull."

In the studio, Mashi and her friend set to work on their sculpture. The friend seemed to be a boy, because he wasn't wearing any bracelets. Mrs. Zinn had told her that was one way of telling boys from girls. Lily was given a lump of clay just to play with, "so you get the feel of it," said Mrs. Zinn, who then left on an errand.

Sitting quietly in a corner with her clay, Lily was able to watch what was going on in the studio. One rather ugly woman with a big mole on her large nose was working vigorously on a mound of clay, slapping and smoothing it. Sweat glistened on her face and bare muscular arms. She wheezed as she worked, and her thin breasts drooped and swayed. Lily felt sorry for her because she was so unattractive. But the woman herself was completely absorbed in her work.

Just then a man came in. His long curls flowed down his back. He ran up to the ugly woman and they hugged and kissed. They talked in a low whisper for a few minutes, gazing into each others' eyes. Then the man left and the woman went back to molding her clay.

Lily felt a thrill of understanding go through her. So this is what it meant to be in a place where women and men were equal! She wished she had a video camera. She'd show this scene to all the girls in her class who tried on lipstick in the school bathroom, behind their mothers' backs, and talked about which guy they hoped would notice them. And she'd show the scene to all the guys who only noticed girls who wore lipstick!

Lily watched Mashi and her friend. Mashi seemed to be doing most of the talking, adding more clay onto the lump the boy was working on, giving him tips on how to pinch and roll and mold. Mashi's manner might even be considered bossy in Lily's school. But here, the boy seemed happy to be working with Mashi, and smiled at her.

Lily felt herself smiling too. This was wonderful! What if her school were like this, where girls and boys were friends and boys didn't think it was "sissy" to take directions from a girl? Then she wouldn't have to spend time arguing about whether girls were better than boys.

Lily knew she had to tell the Queen and Phyra about the destruction of Crete. If they could prevent Crete from being destroyed, history would be changed forever. Then maybe when Lily got back home, life would be totally different. Mom wouldn't have to put up with her lousy boss, who kept giving the men more money than he gave Mom. And maybe Lauren wouldn't be so obsessed with clothes and whether her thighs were too fat to wear a mini-skirt. And maybe Lily herself wouldn't have to put up with Chuck anymore.

Lily knew where to find the Queen. The only problem was—she didn't know the language! And she couldn't ask Mrs. Zinn to help, since Mrs. Zinn had forbidden her to tell the Queen what she knew about the invasion. Lily made up her mind to try hard to learn Cretan.

Chapter 11

The Suspicious Character

*M*ashi held out a brown, misshapen piece of fungi. Lily accepted it and popped it into her mouth. Mmm! Mushroomy!

Her eyelids were heavy as they sat sunning themselves at the edge of the forest. She could feel a contented smile on her face. Her mind was blank and sleepy. She knew she had been worried about something for the past few days, but she just couldn't recall what it was now. Their baskets beside them were full of wild plants. Lily had been nibbling all morning on whatever Mashi offered her—juicy stalks, or sour leaves, or spicy, slightly bitter roots—she tried them all. At first she'd been afraid to taste what looked like weeds to her—who knew if they were poisonous? But Mashi bit fearlessly into everything she gathered.

Once Lily had reached for a plant with clusters of tiny white flowers and feathery leaves, much like something they'd just gathered. She was about to put it into her mouth when Mashi glanced at her and grabbed her arm. Her eyes were wide. She scolded Lily loudly and threw the plant aside. Since then Lily only ate what Mashi gave her.

"Ouch!" Lily shouted. Her arm was being stung. She looked down and saw she'd leaned on the home of some red ants. She jumped up and brushed at herself frantically. She hoped they hadn't crawled into her clothes! Mashi was giggling and rolling on the ground. "I hope they bite you too!" Lily said, even though she knew Mashi couldn't understand English. That just made Mashi laugh even more. She thought English sounded funny.

Then Mashi lifted her head and peered around. She reached for a plant, plucked off a leaf, and rubbed it on Lily's arm. The pain went away! Lily was amazed at how much Mashi knew about plants.

The stinging ants had awakened her from her drowsiness. She remembered her quest to tell the Queen what she knew, and started in again on learning the Cretan language. She pointed to the ants and looked at Mashi for the word in her language. "Ants," Mashi said in Cretan. Lily pinched herself. "Bite," replied Mashi. "The ants are biting you."

"The ants are biting you," Lily copied.

Mashi laughed again. "No, you should say, 'The ants are biting *me*.'"

"The ants are biting *me*," obeyed Lily. She wasn't sure what the difference was.

"Good," said Mashi. "Good," said Lily.

They picked up their baskets and wandered into the forest. They'd been out all day, walking farther and farther away from home. Lily had learned the names of lots of plants and animals. They saw shepherds and sheep, and other people gathering plants.

But now there was no one else around. Lily kept having the urge to look over her shoulder to see if someone suspicious was following them. Mashi didn't seem to be afraid at all, though.

The path through the forest was clear and well-used. The trees were small and growing close together, with lots of brush. But as they walked deeper, it grew dim. Tall trees towered around them. The sunlight through the leaves made a green glow. Lily could see everything clearly despite the leafy canopy: fuzzy, soft, pretty green moss covered everything, and ferns waved gently on the ground between the trees. Lily stood still, gazing up and around.

Mashi had walked on ahead, and when Lily

looked up the path she couldn't see her. She started walking, then heard—crickle...crickle ...crickle—a faint sound behind her. She held her breath and kept walking quietly. Crickle...crickle .... Someone was following her! Who was it? Where was Mashi? She turned around quickly and looked behind her—an empty path. Was someone lurking behind a tree, waiting to jump out at her? She ran up the path. "Mashi!" she shouted.

She heard her name within the trees, and stopped. Mashi was squatting on the ground scooping nuts into her basket. She smiled and pointed to the nuts and to Lily's basket.

As Lily knelt down to fill her basket, she heard it again. Crickle...crickle. She turned, and saw a little brown chipmunk nosing around the ground. Lily smiled and sighed in relief, and watched the animal at work. Its tiny paws found a nut, and it sat up to examine it. Then its black eyes saw Lily and Mashi. Panic paralyzed it for half a second. It dropped the nut and raced away, its white stomach flat against the ground.

Chapter 12

The Ship

"*T*ell me again what happened to destroy Crete," Lily said to Mrs. Zinn. They were walking down to the dock with Inasha and Mashi to see a ship come in. Lily had decided she needed more information to put her plan into action. She hoped her request sounded offhanded, like she was just asking it to pass the time.

"Why do you want to know that?" Mrs. Zinn asked sternly. She wasn't fooled at all. "I told you I don't want you to tell anyone here what you know."

"Oh, I won't!" lied Lily. "I was just curious, that's all."

They walked in silence for several more minutes. They passed Inasha's friend Ambi's house, and Inasha stopped in front of the porch and shouted for Ambi. Inasha had a big, loud voice, like a bell or a gong, and she didn't hesitate to use it. In fact, all the Cretan women seemed very loud to Lily. The men were loud too, but that

didn't seem as strange.

Once, Lily remembered, she had shouted back loudly at her social studies teacher, Mr. Hughes. He was always calling her "chica" and wiggling his eyebrows at her. He said she looked Mexican. So one day in class, she said, right in front of everyone else, "My name is Lily. Don't call me 'chica'!" Mr. Hughes had gasped in mock horror and everyone laughed. After class that day, Peter Davis, the handsomest boy in sixth grade, came up to Lily and told her she wasn't a good sport. "Mr. Hughes thinks you're pretty, that's all. You should take it as a compliment," he advised her. Lily could still feel her stomach churning in anger, but she hadn't said anything to Peter.

Ambi appeared and Inasha beckoned her to come along with them. They put their arms around each other and threw their heads back and laughed and sang as they walked along. Ambi was a musician and she knew all sorts of songs. Mashi followed her mother, laughing and singing just as loudly.

Lily felt odd walking along so quietly. Mrs. Zinn must have felt the same, because she started talking.

"I don't know too much about the destruction of Crete because I've never visited then, for obvious reasons. But I do know what archeologists found."

Lily listened as carefully as she could but tried to appear more interested in seeing whether the ship had come in yet.

"As I told you before, it was caused by a flood or an earthquake," Mrs. Zinn continued. "Then Crete, in its weakened state, was invaded by an army, probably from Greece. We know the people who occupied the island next spoke Greek.

"In the Queen's throne rooms, archeologists found a large oil jar, as big as a person, overturned on the ground. Maybe the Queen had tried to protect herself by rolling that huge jar to block the doorway."

Lily's heart felt heavy at the thought of the kind, proud Queen who'd welcomed her into the ceremony, being violently dragged away. Lily hoped the Queen had shouted as loudly as she could.

They were at the beach, and they saw the ship, looking small way out at sea, fold its sails. Lily couldn't wait to see what it would bring—cloth? or jewelry? or animals?

Then Mrs. Zinn said, "That's a Mycenean ship. Those are the people who probably invaded Crete." Lily looked at the toy-sized ship on the sea. Surely, if the Queen knew what was to happen, she'd prepare the Cretan army to fight that little ship, and save Crete!

Chapter 13

The Dance

*O*ne day Lily came home for supper to find that neither Mrs. Zinn nor Mashi's grandmother, Eyla, were there. Lily was surprised, because that night was to be the monthly full moon dance. Mashi and her friends had been teaching Lily the steps, and everyone planned to go.

After supper, people wandered off by twos and threes to the dance, and no one said anything about where Mrs. Zinn and Eyla were. Were they already at the dance? Lily wondered. She and Mashi were put in charge of a couple of Mashi's little cousins for the first part of the dance, so the uncles and aunts could dance freely.

Mashi was wearing some make-up for the occasion. She asked Lily to stand still while she applied red color to Lily's lips, and outlined her eyes in black. Even Edani, Mashi's father, and even the little cousins, were wearing make-up tonight. Mashi combed Lily's hair and put a headband around the crown of her head. She gave Lily a gold necklace and some arm cuffs. Then they ran out with the little cousins and up the long slope to the palace.

The moon was full and bright, and the tall torches on poles made people's faces glow warmly yellow in the dark. People were milling around, greeting each other and admiring new clothes and jewelry. Lily was surprised to see many men and boys in long skirts, like the one she was wearing! No one seemed to think there was anything odd about it. Lily recognized one of the men sailors, a very muscular man, wearing a pretty purple long skirt and a heavy gold necklace on his hairy chest. His hair, usually tied up and out of the way, was left loose to flow over his shoulders. He was actually pretty handsome!

Lily looked around for Mrs. Zinn, but soon got caught up in a game of tag. There were so many children running around, laughing and screeching, that Lily didn't know who she was running from, and whenever someone tagged her they just fell and rolled around and giggled.

As she sat catching her breath, Lily's mind went back to a game of tag she'd been forced into on the playground at school. The girls were playing "four-square," very neatly and quietly bouncing a ball to each other. A few boys, who couldn't get the other boys to let them into the football game at the far end of the playground, stormed the girls, who took off screaming. One girl was caught by the boys and had her shoes taken off and thrown over the fence.

The music started, and Lily was shaken out of her daydream. A boy grabbed Lily's hand and they ran to join a circle. The music was strange to her ears, but fortunately it involved lots of drumming and had a good beat she could follow. They circled right and left, faster and slower, amid the glowing torches, under a black sky cascading with stars. The boys on either side of her smiled at her when they saw she was catching on.

During the slow part of the dance Lily looked around and saw what seemed like hundreds of circles of people spread across the field in front of the palace. Lily could see the Queen, her husband, and some of the priestesses sitting on the palace balcony and watching.

Lily sat out the next dance to take over watching the little cousins from Mashi, and a couple of Mashi's friends sat out with her to keep her company. They sprawled on the cool grass, watching the swirling dancers.

"So do you like it here in Crete?" asked Hala. She spoke slowly so Lily would understand.

"Sure," Lily answered. She was happy she'd picked up enough Cretan to answer.

"Tell us about where you're from," said Nalbi. He was Mashi's pottery partner.

Lily hesitated. She'd told them before that she was from what we now call Lebanon. But they knew more about that place than she did—Nalbi's family on his father's side were sailors and they often went there. She had to say something, though—she didn't want them to suspect she was lying.

Seeing her reluctance to speak, Hala nudged Nalbi and muttered something to him. He said, "I'm sorry if it upsets you to think about your home. Mashi told us what happened there."

"What happened there?" Lily repeated. What did Mashi tell them?

"Yes. She told us you're an orphan—that you have no mother and father. You came to Crete to see if anyone would take you."

"Take me?" said Lily, still mystified.

"Take you as a daughter, or a sister. Mashi is very happy. She wants you to be her sister!" Nalbi smiled at Lily, and put his hand comfortingly on hers.

Lily hadn't known Mashi liked her so much. She wasn't sure where Mashi had gotten that story, but still, it was so nice of her!

The dance lasted late into the night. The round moon climbed up the sky and got smaller, then climbed down again as dawn started to show in the east. Lily danced till she was exhausted, ate heartily at the midnight buffet of crabs and fish, fruits, cheese, and bread—then danced some more.

As morning arrived, she walked home with her arms linked with Mashi's, giggling and yawning. It was like the best party she'd ever been to— no competition to see who was wearing the latest clothes or who looked the cutest—just lots of fun. It was so nice not to have to worry about how much she was eating and whether she was "going off her diet." Everyone here just ate until they were full. Lily felt a new feeling—like she was safe and warm, like she was being gently supported in a hammock of her new friends.

At home she and Mashi sank into their beds and to sleep right away.

Chapter 14

Old Women's Secrets

When Lily woke up it was afternoon, and Mrs. Zinn wasn't beside her on the floor. She stepped into the main room, where Mashi's grandfather was stirring a pot on the fire in the middle of the room.

"Goddess is smiling," he greeted Lily. That's what they said in Crete when it was sunny outside.

Lily sat on a low stool beside him and asked, "Where is Olivia?" That was Mrs. Zinn's first name.

"She went with Eyla to the ceremony," he said. "The old women's ceremony."

"When she come back?" Lily hadn't yet mastered the future tense.

"Hmm," said Grandfather, and kept stirring. He didn't seem to want to say any more. Lily went back into the bedroom. She wondered why Mrs. Zinn hadn't told her where she was going.

Mashi was just beginning to stretch and blink.

"Mashi," Lily shook her. "Olivia at ceremony. With Grandmother. You know that?"

Mashi rubbed her eyes and sat up. "Yes, but we're not really supposed to talk about it. All the old women go to a ceremony when we go to the full-moon dance. It's because they are—" Mashi searched for words Lily would understand—"the moon goddess is not their goddess anymore. They don't have blood when the moon goes away."

Lily gathered that Mashi meant they didn't get their periods anymore. "Where they go?"

"I don't know. You don't find out till you're an old woman." Mashi smiled in anticipation of someday knowing the secret. "We don't know when they'll be back, either."

Lily felt a ripple of fear go through her stomach. How would she manage without Mrs. Zinn? What if she got sick? Or what if Mrs. Zinn never came back?

Mashi got up and shuffled out to the porch, where she sat on the steps and plucked some thyme to chew on. Lily went out and sat beside her. The sun was high above them, but there wasn't the usual afternoon activity on the road—everyone was just getting up after staying out all night.

"What do you want to do today?" Mashi

asked.

"I want to find Olivia," Lily said. She was leaning forward over her knees and staring at the ground.

"Well, we can't do that!" Mashi exclaimed. She plucked another sprig of thyme and, chewing lazily, leaned back and turned her face to the afternoon sun.

"If we find her, what they do to us?" Lily turned to squint at Mashi.

"It would be wrong to look for her. It would bring us bad luck." Mashi looked at Lily and saw how serious and worried she was. "Are you afraid to be without her?"

"Yes. A little."

Mashi scooted closer and put an arm around Lily's waist. "Don't worry. You can be part of our family." They sat in silence for a few minutes. Lily couldn't believe Mrs. Zinn had just left her with no warning! She sighed heavily.

"Come on," Mashi said, standing up and pulling Lily up by the hand. "I'm going to point out where I think they are. Will that make you feel better?"

They walked up the road to the palace. Lily started to cheer up. If they were only in the palace, she was sure she could find them if she needed to.

But Mashi led her around the palace hill until they were facing out to the rest of the island. Mashi pointed to some hills in the distance. "There are some caves in those hills."

"Caves?" Lily didn't know that word yet.

"It's a hole in the rock," Mashi explained. "You walk in, or crawl." Mashi stooped down and squeezed herself into an imaginary crevice. "Then you can stand up sometimes, or just sit down. The rock is around you."

Lily nodded.

"I heard Grandmother talk about those caves once," Mashi went on. "I think that's where they go for their ceremonies. But I'm not sure."

The hills seemed quite far away. "They walk there?"

"I don't know. It would take half a day to walk there. Maybe they take carts. But they don't make any noise, so I guess they do walk." Mashi sat down cross-legged on the grass.

Lily sat down next to her. She had no hope of finding Mrs. Zinn by herself. "They come back, yes?" she said, trying not to sound worried.

"They always have," said Mashi. "Don't worry. You can stay with us. You can be my sister!" Mashi smiled.

Lily tried to smile too. They sat and watched

the grasses rippling in the breeze.

Suddenly they heard shouts and cheering from behind them, coming from the palace. Mashi jumped up. "Come on! I'll show you something!" She ran into the palace with Lily following her.

Mashi led her through the halls and up some stairs onto a balcony. They squeezed themselves through a small crowd on the balcony and looked down. Lily realized she was looking down at the same courtyard she'd found the first day. It looked very different now.

In the middle of the courtyard was a large, snorting bull with long, pointy horns, held by two people with ropes. A young woman stood at one end of the courtyard, with her hands on her hips, facing the bull. She wore a short skirt split at the sides, revealing her long, muscled legs. Her wavy hair hung in a ponytail down her sturdy back. People were milling around her, slapping her back and saying things to her, and she smiled, but was clearly concentrating on whatever she was about to do. She positioned her feet carefully, as though she were starting a race.

Then the bull was released and she ran straight for him. She grabbed his horns and flew into the air as the bull tossed his head. She landed like a circus performer on his back and jumped off. The

crowd in all the balconies cheered. The bull was caught again with ropes, and patted and slapped gently. Then he was led out a door.

Lily felt like she'd seen this somewhere before. Then she remembered—she had! It was like the painting she saw on her first day in Crete, when she'd been lost in the palace.

"They're practicing for the Autumn Festival," said Mashi. "It's pretty hard and dangerous to do that. But she's one of the best."

They watched as another bull was brought in. This time a man tried it. He managed to catch hold of the horns and flip over, but missed the bull's back and fell on the ground heavily. Fortunately they had padded the ground over there with a thick layer of sand. He stood up slowly and brushed himself off, and got a good cheer from the crowd anyway.

"You do that?" Lily asked Mashi.

"Oh, no. My family doesn't do that. You have to be very strong, and you have to practice from when you're a little kid. But Nalbi and I are making a sculpture of a bull for the Festival. You've seen that."

They sat in silence while the next jumper was getting ready. Then Lily said, "The Festival is next week. What I do for the Festival?"

Mashi looked over at her. "What do you want to do?"

"I don't know. I can't make a sculpture. I can't do *that*." She pointed down at the courtyard and laughed.

"No. But you're a good dancer. Why don't you join the dancers? They always have a dance to show off some new steps before the play, in the theater." Lily had seen the theater, connected to the palace by a long walkway.

"OK," said Lily.

Chapter 15

Weak Legs

*L*ily was almost sorry she'd agreed to be in this dance demonstration. The choreographer teaching them, whose name was Grimbo, was a fierce-looking man with thick eyebrows and a frown on his face. He had a limp, and when he showed them the steps Lily had trouble figuring out what he was doing. She also couldn't understand the names of some movements. When she did things wrong, which she often did, he shouted and came over to her, grabbing her arms and legs roughly and positioning them correctly. She hated to have him touch her.

After the first practice she thought about quitting, but she really wanted to do something for the Festival. One of the dances was especially nice. It was just for women and girls, and it involved lots of graceful waving of arms and slow turns. Only Lily always seemed to be waving when the others were turning.

She didn't know what to do. She couldn't

blame Grimbo for having a limp or for the fact that she couldn't understand him.

The second day went no better. Everyone else seemed to have picked up the steps overnight, except her. She struggled to keep up, but she just felt like she was being pulled along by the circle of dancers, and tripping over her own feet. She felt bad for holding the others back.

As she trudged home after practice, she felt like screaming. How could Mrs. Zinn have left her alone? And why did Mashi suggest she join the dancers? She should have known Lily was nowhere near good enough. She blinked her eyes, and a few hot tears escaped. She wished Mashi could be with her, but she was too busy working on her sculpture.

She heard footsteps running behind her, but she was too embarrassed to turn around. She grabbed her hanky and pretended to blow her nose so she could wipe away the tears unnoticed.

Someone put their arm around her. Lily turned to see Hala, Mashi's friend, smiling at her. She was one of the dancers too.

"You're having trouble with the steps," Hala said. "Want me to help you?"

Before Lily could answer, she burst into tears. She was surprised at her own distress. Hala put both arms around her while she sobbed briefly on her shoulder. Then Lily stepped back and said,

"I don't like Grimbo. He's mean!"

"He looks scary, doesn't he?" said Hala. "I don't like him too much either. My grandfather said he's sour because the Goddess gave him a limp after he was one of the best dancers. He used to go across the sea to perform!"

Lily sighed. She'd try harder to like Grimbo. At least *she* didn't have a limp.

"But Lily," Hala said, "that doesn't mean it's right for him to get angry at you. Just shout back at him! Don't let him move your arms and legs if you don't want him to. Stand still and refuse to move."

Lily was surprised at Hala's solution. "But...is that right? Won't Inasha scold me for shouting at the teacher?"

Hala looked confused. "Why should she scold you? She'd only get upset if you *didn't* show him he can't treat you like that."

Lily smiled in amazement. She sure was glad she was in Crete, and not at home! She and Hala went to the garden at Hala's house, and Lily slowly learned the steps and their names.

The next day, Lily could hardly wait to start practice. She wanted to show everyone how good she was. She arrived early at the theater, when the musicians were still milling around and plinking their lyres lazily. As she was sitting on the steps, she realized Grimbo was walking up to her, leaning heavily on his cane with each step. She stiffened. Would he talk to her? What should she say?

He stopped in front of her and, standing there, seemed to tower above her.

"I hope you do better today than yesterday, Lily!" he said gruffly. He turned and started to limp away without waiting for an answer.

Lily's heart was beating fast. Should she reply? His grumpiness was so annoying, but she felt sorry for him because he couldn't walk very well. She remembered what Hala said, and was about to open her mouth and tell him what she thought, when one of the musicians strolled up to him and started talking. Lily let out her breath in relief. She was almost glad she didn't have to stand up for herself.

She took her place among the dancers. She realized her legs were still shaking a little from nervousness about answering Grimbo. The music started, and the circle of dancers seemed suddenly to lurch into motion. Right away Lily tripped over her feet. Her face flushed hot in embarrassment. She *knew* this dance—it was just the simple warm-up dance! She made herself concentrate on her feet, and for a few minutes she was fine. Then she happened to look up and see that Grimbo was glaring at her. Before she knew it, her chin was trembling and her eyes were watering. She could hardly see the ground.

The music stopped, and Lily found Grimbo hulking over her.

"You are ruining my dance!" he shouted at her. "Why did you decide to join the dancers if you can't dance?" Then, grumbling almost to himself, he said, "The Goddess gave me a limp. And now she gives me a limp in my circle of dancers too." He eased himself to the ground and, kneeling there, grabbed Lily's ankles.

That did it. "Stop that!" Lily shouted. "I've been practicing. I know the steps! But your shouting makes me nervous. Just leave me alone!"

Grimbo looked up at her. Then he gave his hand to the dancer next to Lily, who helped him up, and hobbled away.

Lily's heart felt light, and a smile bubbled up to her face. She caught Hala's eyes across the circle. Hala was smiling too.

As the music started again and Lily's feet started to skip and step in time to the rhythm, she could feel that her knees were still a little shaky. But they felt strong too.

Chapter 16

The Return

"*H*op in back, Lily, and let's go!" Inasha's brother was over to help Grandfather take some food to the palace for the supper. They loaded the cart, and Lily climbed in. As they bumped along the road, Lily's heart beat with excitement. The sky was just beginning to lighten, and she could see the sun rising behind the palace. She'd been practicing and waiting for this day.

Inasha had awakened them when it was still dark that morning. Now Lily was going to help decorate the theater, and then she'd come back, take a bath, get dressed, and the Festival would start!

After the day she stood up to Grimbo he'd left her alone, and now she was just as good a dancer as anyone else. On the last day of practice, Grimbo had even come up to her and said, "Lily, you've improved. I hope you'll be in the Winter Festival." Lily found herself hoping she

would, too, even though she knew she'd probably be back home by then.

She jumped out of the cart at the open-air
theater and waved good-bye to Grandfather and
Uncle. Already people had started hanging up
olive branches and bunches of grapes, and burning incense to make the air smell sweet. Lily's job
was to make sure all the steps, which were also
seats, were clean of bird droppings. She and Hala
grabbed large clam shells to scrape away any droppings, and ran into the seating area.

The air was vibrating with excitement. The
theater couldn't hold that many people on the
long steps that surrounded it, so a lot of people
had staked out their spot by spending the night.
There were to be five performances of the play,
each one preceded by the dance Lily was in, so as
many people as possible could see it. People
laughed and sang, and a light breeze blew wafts
of incense around Lily. She and Hala took turns
running down to the stage to wheedle small hand-
fuls of grapes from the people hanging them up.
Lily got so hot that she took her shirt off. So what
if her stomach was a little pudgy!

On her way home Lily stopped by the pottery
studio to pick up Mashi. They ate a big breakfast, then bathed and dressed and put on make-

up, and waited on the front steps for everyone else to get ready.

"Hurry up!" Mashi shouted. She and Lily were holding hands and skipping in place. Mashi was nervous about whether her sculpture would win a prize.

Just then Mashi stood still and turned her head to one side, listening. Lily listened too, and heard far-away strumming on a lyre, and faint drumbeats. Mashi dropped Lily's hands and took off in a run. "They're back! Come on, Lily!"

Lily followed, a little sorry to get sweaty again before the dance, but too curious not to run as fast as she could.

At the top of the palace hill they met a large group of people, walking and singing in a long, amorphous column snaking across the countryside. Lily realized it was the old women! She and Mashi searched for Eyla and Mrs. Zinn. Dozens of women passed them: tall and short, fat and thin, muscular and graceful. Other people were also waiting with Lily and Mashi, and when they saw the women they were looking for, they cheered and ran to them. All the old women looked happy, with calm smiles and sparkling, deep eyes. Finally, they spotted Eyla and Mrs. Zinn. Lily noticed their cheeks were rosier than usual.

"You got back just in time!" said Mashi as she hugged her grandmother.

"Yes, I'm glad you're back!" Lily added. She put her arm around Mrs. Zinn as they all walked home.

When they reached the front door, Mrs. Zinn said, "Lily, you've become a real Cretan! You haven't spoken one word of English to me!"

Lily was surprised to realize it was true!

"I was feeling badly that I'd left you with no warning," Mrs. Zinn continued in English. "But our ritual is a secret, and I see you're doing fine. I think we'll be going back home soon—maybe even tomorrow. So you should probably say your good-byes today." Mrs. Zinn stepped inside to wash up.

Lily was stunned. Mashi saw her distress and asked, "What did she say? Tell me!"

Lily didn't know what to tell Mashi. She couldn't leave without talking to the Queen. But besides that, to say good-bye to all her friends! And she thought she could become a dance teacher for the small children if she stayed a little longer. She felt…*important* in Crete. How could she leave so soon?

Chapter 17

The Decision

*L*ily wanted to talk to Mrs. Zinn, but she was so busy either dancing or helping out with the play that she couldn't get away. She knew Mrs. Zinn had gone to watch the bull games after she saw the dance and the play. Finally, after the last dance performance, Lily slipped away to the palace.

She could hear the crowds cheering as one athlete after another flipped into the air and landed on the bull's back. But she didn't know exactly where Mrs. Zinn was sitting. A man walked out as she stood there puzzling over what to do.

"You look confused," he said.

"I want to find my friend. She's in there somewhere, but I don't know where."

"You'll never get in there now," he said. "Just wait till tomorrow, when things are back to normal. It's impossible to find people during a Festival!"

But tomorrow would be too late, Lily thought.

They might be back home by tomorrow!

The man saw Lily biting her lip. "You want to see her right away, don't you?" he asked. "What kind of woman is she? Old? Young? What work does her family do?"

"She's an old woman. She just came back with all the other old women. She's a guest of Inasha and Eyla, who are palace potters."

"Then, stand by the south door of the palace," the man said. "She's probably sitting with the Queen and the priestesses. She'll come out this door in time for supper."

The sun was on the west side before the bull games were over. People streamed out of the palace. Finally, among the last trickle of people, Mrs. Zinn wandered out arm-in-arm with Phyra, the head priestess.

Lily was almost afraid to disturb them. But if she didn't, it would be too late.

"Mrs. Zinn! I have to talk to you!"

"Phyra, I'll talk to you later," Mrs. Zinn said. She put her arm around Lily and gave her a little squeeze. "Shall we walk to that rock over there?"

Lily realized again how nice it was to be taken seriously. Mrs. Zinn would stop talking to Phyra for her! They sat on a flat rock warmed by the sun.

"Mrs. Zinn, we can't leave Crete yet."

"Why not? We've been here a long time already. We don't want to wear out our welcome."

"Well…" Lily wasn't sure if she should tell Mrs. Zinn the real reason. But she needed Mrs. Zinn's help to accomplish her task. She just had to tell her the truth and really let her know how important this was.

"I know you don't want me to tell people here that they're going to be destroyed," Lily began. "But everyone is so nice! They give us food and clothes and a place to stay, and they're so friendly. How can I leave without warning them? I want you to help me tell the Queen or Phyra what you know. They'd never believe me alone and besides, I can't speak well enough."

Mrs. Zinn was silent. She looked at Lily, then down at the rock. "Lily, I can't do that," she said finally. "I've taken a vow not to do anything to change history. In fact, I shouldn't have even brought us here—it's a disruption. But sometimes I just need to come here where old women like me are respected. It renews me. But we certainly can't do anything more than that. The Cretans must do the best they can. If we try to help them we may cause more harm than good. They know their own strength better than we do. They have one of the best navies around, with strong men and women ready to defend Crete. So let's leave it to them." Mrs. Zinn put her hand over Lily's.

Lily stared down at Mrs. Zinn's hand. Then she looked up at the palace and the rolling landscape. She saw some big bonfires flare up and heard people cheer. And she knew what she wanted to do.

"Then, Mrs. Zinn," she said, looking into her eyes, "I don't want to go home. I want to stay in Crete. Mashi said I could live with her and be her sister."

"But, Lily!" Mrs. Zinn leaned forward and her brow was wrinkled. "Why would you want to do that? Don't you miss your parents? Don't you miss your friends?"

"I guess I'd miss them for a while. But I have new friends here. And I can go wherever I want, even into the forest by myself. I can say anything I want, and be loud, and no one gets upset. I can be friends with boys and they don't make fun of me. And I get to do grown-up things, like make pottery and go dancing."

Mrs. Zinn looked at her quietly. Lily was glad she'd thought of this solution to her problem. Her heart felt lighter already. She saw Mashi waving to her and got down off the rock to join her for dinner around a bonfire.

Chapter 18

The Seeds

*M*rs. Zinn held out a handful of tiny brown objects. "You're sure you want to stay, Lily, even after all we've just talked about?"

Lily nodded. They were sitting in one of the olive groves farthest from the town, the day after the Festival. Mrs. Zinn had just been telling her all the disadvantages of staying in Crete—she'd have to become a potter like Inasha and couldn't choose her own career; she'd have to live with all sorts of relatives and wouldn't have much privacy; she could never again read a book or see a movie (Lily hadn't thought of that—would it bother her?); and most of all, she'd miss her parents.

"Here's what I'm going to do," Mrs. Zinn continued. "I'll take these seeds back with me and sprout them. Then in a few weeks I can come back—these living objects can transport me to Crete a few weeks from now. In the time it takes them to grow, an equal amount of time will have passed here in Crete. You can tell me then whether you've changed your mind, and I'll bring you back if you want."

Lily ran her finger over the small round seeds. "Are you sure it will work? What if they don't sprout?"

"If you're worried about that, you'd better come back with me now. I've told you I'm completely against your staying here. But I can't take you back unless you want to go and you put your mind to it. I'm taking these seeds as a precaution—I'd hate for you to be stranded here with no way to go home. But yes, there is the possibility that it won't work."

Lily thought about this possibility. Was she really sure she wanted to stay? When she'd told Mashi at dinner the night before, Mashi had hugged her and they danced around—Mashi was happier than when she'd won her prize! But still—what if Lily did miss her parents too much?

"If it doesn't work," Lily asked, "what will you do?"

"I'll have to leave you here, I guess. Or, if I came back using the green coin, I'd land here at the same time we both landed at first. And since you wouldn't be with me, it would be like you were never here—you'd be at home with your parents, and you wouldn't know anything about this trip."

This logic was a little confusing to Lily. But she knew she didn't want to lose her memory of her time in Crete. "Then don't do that, Mrs. Zinn."

"I won't. In fact, I plan to leave the coin here and not even take it with me. I'm taking other things from today back home—so I could come back to this particular time—although I suppose you would never want to go home at this time."

Lily thought she understood this, and nodded. "Mrs. Zinn, can't you stay just a few more days? Maybe I'd be ready to come home then."

"If I stay, it would only be to give you more time to figure out how to tell the Queen what you know. And I want no part of that."

Lily had to admit she was right—that was the reason she wanted to stay a few more days. There seemed to be no solution but to let Mrs. Zinn go and hope that she wouldn't regret her decision.

"I'll go now." Mrs. Zinn stood up. She'd already said good-bye to Inasha, Eyla, and all her friends, and had convinced them it would be bad luck to go down to the harbor to see her off. She looked hard at Lily one last time. She held out her hand for a handshake and Lily took it. She pressed Lily's hand between both of her own. "Good luck," she said softly.

Chapter 19

The Dream

*L*ily sat straight up in bed and screamed. Mashi jerked awake and rolled over.

"What's wrong? Lily, wake up!"

Inasha and Edani appeared at the doorway with a lamp. They both sat down on the mattress on the floor. By now Lily was awake, looking bewildered at the crowd in her bedroom. "What happened?"

Inasha pressed her hands on either side of Lily's head to bring her back to herself. "You were screaming. Did you have a dream?"

Lily looked around blinking for several seconds. She took a deep breath and let it out. "Yes. A bad dream." She stared at the spiral designs on the bedspread, following the circles in and out with her eyes. Mashi, Inasha, and Edani sat quietly watching her.

"Tell us what it was," urged Inasha. "It's not good to keep things to yourself."

"All right," Lily agreed. "But…" she looked

Inasha in the eyes, "it was really scary. I don't want to upset you."

"Don't worry about us, just start talking!" said Mashi.

Lily traced the designs on the bedspread with her finger. "I was down at the dock. I think Mashi was with me. But it was hard to tell. We were adults. We were just taking a walk. Suddenly, we felt the ground shake. We thought it was an earthquake. The sky got darker, and I looked out to sea and saw a huge, huge ship. It filled the sky up, it was so big. It was blocking the sun. Its sails weren't white. They looked red—like they were dyed with blood. And there were people on the ship—they were huge too. They were all men with dirty hair and beards, and they were pointing giant swords and arrows at us. Mashi and I started running up the beach. But the ship was so big it made a huge wave roll on top of us. We were pulled out to sea by the waves. We were drowning.

"Then suddenly, we were on the ship, in a small, dark room. There were so many of those giant men looking at us. They said, 'We are going to kill you all and destroy your palace! Your Goddess can't protect you!' Mashi and I were crying and calling to the Goddess, and—"

Inasha made a quick gasping sound and Lily looked up at her. Inasha's eyes were wide, and her face was white. When she noticed Lily looking at her, she pressed her finger to her upper lip and took a deep breath.

"That's enough for now, Lily." Inasha's voice was shaking just a little. "You rest and try to remember as much of the dream as you can. In the morning, I think we'll go see a friend of mine. She knows all about dreams."

Mashi grabbed her mother's arm. "What does it mean? Is that going to happen to me and Lily?" Mashi's eyes were terrified as she clung to her mother. Edani was also clutching Inasha's hand.

Inasha stood up. "Mashi, I want you to be strong. Fear never solves anything. Help Lily remember her dream till morning." Inasha and Edani left with their arms around each other.

Chapter 20

In the Apple Orchard

*L*ily hurried to keep up with Inasha's long strides. She wasn't sure where they were going. Inasha seemed almost to have forgotten Lily was with her. She said nothing as they walked. Her eyes were focused straight ahead.

Suddenly, Inasha stopped at an orchard of apple trees. She sat down on a rock, and Lily sat down beside her. Still Inasha said nothing. Her large, muscular hands and sensitive, long fingers were spread flat on her knees. She closed her eyes and breathed deeply. Lily thought she saw her lower lip tremble, as though she were about to burst into tears.

"Lily, I must tell you," she began. "What you saw in your dream—it wasn't just a scary dream for you alone. You received that dream from the Goddess. She is telling us something through your dream." She looked at Lily to see if she understood. Lily raised her eyebrows in reply, meaning, "Yes, I understand. Go on."

"Lily, I don't want to alarm you," Inasha continued slowly, looking at Lily with sad, deep eyes. "But since you were chosen for this dream, I'll tell you the whole story. The Goddess has been sending us very similar messages for many years— even before Mashi was born. The priestesses received visions that our palace would be destroyed, that people who didn't care about the Goddess would come here and kill us. Most people don't know about these visions because the Queen is keeping it quiet until she can decide what these visions really mean, and what to do about them. But I know—I work in the palace, and I talk to the priestesses. I've known for a long time."

Inasha again looked at Lily. This time Lily's forehead was furrowed. She was confused. "Does Mashi know this? Does Edani?"

"No. Only me and my mother. I don't talk about it with anyone. I want to wait until the Queen is ready."

That explained why Mrs. Zinn didn't know. Lily had so carefully planned her strategy—thinking up what the dream would be about, planning a night to scream. She'd hoped Inasha would believe a dream, since Cretans put so much faith in visions. That way, Lily wouldn't have to go into the whole story of time-traveling and how she knew about the destruction.

Lily had been delighted when her idea had worked so well. Inasha had been convinced of the dream's importance with almost no effort on Lily's part. But now Lily understood why—Inasha knew all along! Even the Queen knew! And they still hadn't been able to prevent the invasion. Lily's head was spinning. She didn't know what to do.

"Come on, let's go before you forget your dream." Inasha stood up and strode back to the road.

"Where are we going?" Lily scrambled up and ran after her.

"We're going to the Queen, to tell her about your dream. Don't be scared," she added when she saw Lily's wide eyes and open mouth. "I'll be with you. Come on!" she urged again, when Lily stalled.

Chapter 21

The Queen's Counsel

The lion-with-bird's-head creatures were staring at Lily. She and Inasha stood before the Queen, who was seated on her throne. A few other people were waiting in the outer room, sitting on the benches. That's where Lily and Inasha had been just a minute ago, before one of the Queen's helpers had called them in and shut the big wooden doors.

The Queen smiled at them from her seat. "Tell me what you need," she said.

Inasha looked at Lily. *She* was obviously not going to do any talking—Lily had to do it all. Lily's throat felt dry, and her tongue felt thick. The red and white walls of the room seemed to vibrate with expectation. Everyone was silent, watching her.

What should she do? They were so kind to her. She couldn't lie to them! Should she tell them the whole story about being a time-traveler and only wanting to help them? But they might not

understand. And Mrs. Zinn might never be allowed to come back to this place where old women were respected. No—she just had to play along a little longer.

"I had a dream," she began softly, looking at her toes.

"Look at the Queen, Lily," Inasha reminded her. "It's not friendly to look away. And speak up! Let's hear what you have to say."

So Lily told the whole dream, with somewhat less enthusiasm than before. When she finished, the Queen was silent. She didn't look scared the way Inasha had done. She sat looking ahead of her, thinking, for a few minutes. Lily's breath was shallow, and her fists were clenched, waiting to hear what the Queen would say.

Finally the Queen said, "Inasha, I want to talk to Lily alone." Inasha turned and walked to the door, pushed it open, and was gone. Lily was alone with the Queen. Her stomach was starting to cramp from nervousness.

The Queen stood up and brought two low stools to Lily. They both sat down, and the Queen took Lily's hands in her own. Lily looked into her deep brown eyes and felt calmer.

"It's good you want to help us, Lily," the Queen began slowly. "I've known since I first saw you that you're a good person." She paused, and continued to look at Lily. "I don't know where you're from. But it's someplace very far away."

Lily smiled in relief. The Queen wasn't angry at her! But she felt as though the Queen were looking right into her.

"As you saw in your dream, Crete will probably be destroyed," the Queen continued. "I don't know if anything can be done. The visions are so strong. Inasha may have told you we've had many other visions like yours."

"Yes," Lily whispered. Then, remembering to speak loudly, she said, "Isn't there anything you can do? What about all your weapons, and all the strong fighters?"

"We'll be as prepared as we can," said the Queen.

Lily couldn't believe there was nothing more to be done. The Queen just didn't realize how serious this was. She didn't realize that the whole world would be taken over by people who thought women were inferior to men!

Lily made one last effort. "I can't tell you how I know, but you must believe me—if this palace is destroyed, the Goddess will be forgotten! Women will be treated like they aren't as good as men!"

"I know," said the Queen. "We can already see that all around us. The ships that come here to trade with us have no women sailors. I've heard that some people keep women at home all the time. I really don't know how they manage that." The Queen waved her hand in disbelief, then continued. "Remember one thing, Lily—the Goddess may be forgotten by most people, but she's always there for you, no matter how far away from Crete you are."

Lily nodded. That was it, then. There was nothing more to say. The United States would not magically treat women equally if Lily went back. Well, at least she could stay in Crete forever if she wanted. She tried to extract her hands from the Queen's grip to get up and leave. But the Queen held on.

"One more thing, Lily," she said. Her warm brown eyes seemed to penetrate Lily's. "I want you to go back home."

Lily felt like she'd been swatted. "You don't want me here?"

"We like you. And Mashi loves you like a sister. But even though you may be too young to understand this, you have work to do at home. I see that you will help women and men work together again. If you stay here, you can't do that. I don't know how you get home, but the next chance you get, you should take it." The Queen gave Lily's hands a final squeeze, then stood up and picked up her stool. Lily did the same.

"The Goddess is with you, Lily," the Queen said as she put her stool away and seated herself on her throne again.

"Yes," said Lily. I'll sure need all the help I can get, she thought to herself as she pushed open the door and walked out.

Chapter 22

The Moon Over Crete

*T*he waiting turned out to be the hardest part. She and Mashi were weeding the garden, which she normally hated to do. Now, it seemed interminable: pull out a weed, look around for another, pull out a weed, look around for another. Would she be doing this every week of her life? Or would she one day see her parents again, and be able to do the work the Queen talked about? Every hour she prayed that Mrs. Zinn's seeds sprouted, and that she could return to Crete to get Lily.

When she had walked out of the throne room a week ago—was that all?—it seemed like months—she'd thought it would be hard to decide whether to leave Crete or stay. But within hours, her decision became crystal-clear: if she and Mrs. Zinn were the only people who knew what it was like to live in a place that respected women and treated them equally, she *had* to go back. She had to let other girls know they didn't just have to put up with whatever they got.

Now all she could do was wait. All the things she'd enjoyed before were just ways to pass the time till Mrs. Zinn arrived. Even wandering in the forest made her sad because she knew it would be cut down by the invaders, and Crete would become rocky and wind-swept.

Mashi and Inasha knew she was waiting for Mrs. Zinn. They knew the Queen had told Lily she must leave Crete. Mashi cried and clung to Lily when she'd heard. Even Inasha seemed sad. But knowing she might never see them again wasn't even as hard as waiting, and not knowing if or when Mrs. Zinn would arrive.

Lily started thinking about what her life would be like at home, now that she had been to Crete. If she got home it would be time for her flute lesson on Saturday. She was pretty sure she could talk Mrs. Zinn out of that! Then on Monday she'd go to school again. Lily felt shivers of anticipation up her spine at just the thought of seeing her school and friends again. But then she remembered—Chuck might be at the bus stop again—and he'd give her another dirty picture. What would she do?

Lily wondered why she felt so furious by the pictures that Chuck gave her, but not by seeing all the topless women in Crete. What was the difference? The women and girls in Crete weren't just lying on a bed gazing into the camera. They were in charge of things. And they didn't wear tops because they didn't see any reason to if they weren't cold—just like men. Besides, Chuck was giving her the pictures just to upset her—he knew she hated it.

As they were weeding, Lily decided to ask Mashi what to do about Chuck. Mashi had just gone to refill her bucket of water. When she came back, Lily said, "Mashi, what would you do if there was a boy who was bothering you—" Lily didn't even know how to describe her problem, because she'd never seen any pictures like that in Crete—"if he was doing something that made you really mad, and even when you told him to stop, he wouldn't?"

Mashi looked puzzled. "Why wouldn't he stop if you told him to?"

"I don't know. He just wouldn't."

Mashi dipped a clay cup into the bucket and poured water gently on some onions. "Well...I would tell other people. Like my mother, or someone older in the pottery studio."

"What if they couldn't get him to stop either? What if older people told you not to worry about what the boy was doing? What if people even told you that you should like him?"

Mashi opened her eyes wide, then started to laugh. "That would never happen. How could I like someone who was being mean to me? Anyway, of course the boy would stop bothering me, especially if I told my mother or someone else. He would be too embarrassed not to. He would have no friends if he behaved like that."

Lily wished she could laugh with Mashi, but she felt sad to think that boys in her school weren't embarrassed at all to be caught bothering girls—in fact she could imagine Chuck bragging about what he had done. Lily decided then and there that even if Lauren wouldn't support her, even if the teachers wouldn't support her, she was just going to keep telling people about the rotten things Chuck did until she found *someone* at her school who would stand up with her and make Chuck stop.

A cart rumbled past them. They looked up to see it was filled with barrels, on its way to the palace storeroom.

"What's in there?" Mashi called.

"Apple cider. Want some?" said the cart driver. She stopped the ox pulling the cart, and scooped out two dipperfuls of cider for them. As they drank the sweet juice, the driver said to Mashi,

"I saw your mother's friend Olivia Zinn just now."

Mashi and Lily both stopped drinking. "Where is she?" Lily gasped.

"Sitting on Ambi's porch. She wasn't gone very long, was she?" The driver started the ox up and the cart rolled away.

Lily and Mashi tore down the road to Ambi's. Mrs. Zinn was sitting in the shade, chatting and laughing with Ambi's mother. Lily and Mashi ran up to her and threw their arms around her.

"I'm so glad to see you!" Lily shouted.

"You've certainly changed your mind since I last saw you," Mrs. Zinn remarked in English.

"The Queen says I have to go home. I have work to do there!" Lily said proudly.

"So you've talked to the Queen." Mrs. Zinn's lips were pressed together, and her eyes looked worried.

"Yes, but it's OK. I'll tell you all about it later. Now let's go home!"

"Not so fast. I have to at least put in an appearance at Inasha's house."

So Lily had one last supper in Crete. Mashi cried at first, but then she decided that Lily would have to come back for the Winter Festival and the Spring Festival. "I don't know if I can," said Lily. "Try to," Mashi cajoled, squeezing Lily's arm.

They decided to leave right after the meal. Lily gave Mashi back her clothes and put her own skirt on again. She felt sad at not looking like a Cretan anymore.

As she and Mrs. Zinn walked to the beach, the setting sun shone over the low houses, and through the trees in the orchard. Lily felt a lump in her throat, and her chin trembled. She turned to look back at the palace one last time. Above its familiar walls, the round moon had appeared, glowing softly in the blue sky.

No matter where I am, Lily thought, I can look at the same moon that shone over Crete.

Afterword

Was There Really a Place Where Women and Men Were Considered Equal?

*A*rcheologists began unearthing the ruins of the palace in Crete during the first part of this century. So far four palaces have been found in different parts of Crete. The palace Lily visits is in Knossos—you can tour the ruins if you go to Crete (which is now part of Greece.) Be aware, though, that the tour guides might not know that many people think the palace culture used to be egalitarian!

When archeologists found the palaces, they were amazed at their technological advancement. They found evidence of underground pipes to carry water, and bathtubs and flush toilets in the living quarters of the palace. They also found paved roads and evidence of trade with other cultures. But most of all, the archeologists were impressed by the beauty of the many paintings on the walls, and the fragments of pottery, jewelry, and sculpture they found.

All along, people have noticed that some of

the paintings and seals depict women and men in similar roles. Both genders participated in the dangerous "bull games," and both were shown dancing, or carrying gifts, or worshipping. Many statues of women holding snakes or double-headed axes were found, and these are thought to be goddess figures. Some paintings showed men and boys with long hair, dressed in long skirts and wearing jewelry. We can tell the men and women apart in the paintings because the men were painted red and the women white.

In the throne room, archeologists noted the absence of grandeur and the importance of nature; even the throne seemed "plant-like" with its wavy-edged back. This is very unlike most male-dominated cultures, in which nature is to be conquered, not revered.

Yet despite all these signs of an egalitarian, peaceful, and nature-loving lifestyle, scholars generally continue to think the Cretan ruler was a king. In fact, this period in Cretan history is referred to as the "Minoan" period, after King Minos, a ruler of Crete in a Greek myth. And, beyond mentioning the fact that Cretan women must have enjoyed a high status in society, scholars don't talk about the culture as being egalitarian.

Recently, however, some women scholars have been re-examining the evidence and have concluded there is very good reason to believe that "Minoan" Crete was a goddess-worshipping society in which women held equal if not greater status. Unfortunately, we have very little writing from "Minoan" Crete, and what we do have hasn't been deciphered yet.

Here is a book for you and your parents or teachers to read:

The Chalice and the Blade: Our History, Our Future, by Riane Eisler (Harper & Row, 1987). This book talks not only about Crete, but also about much older prehistoric European cultures that are also thought to be goddess-worshipping and egalitarian.

You might also want to look up books on Minoan Crete to see color pictures of the beautiful frescos (wall paintings) found in the palaces. Many have been restored by artists from the fragments archeologists found, so you can see what they might have looked like to Lily.

You could also subscribe, or get your school or neighborhood library to subscribe, to a magazine for girls, that's edited by girls. It has stories, comics, games, and articles:

New Moon: The Magazine for Girls and Their Dreams, P.O. Box 3587, Duluth, MN 55803. Or call 218-728-5507.